Disney · PIXAR

LUCA

Published in the United States by Random House Children's Books, a division of Penguin Random House LLC, 1745 Broadway, New York, NY 10019, and in Canada by Penguin Random House Canada Limited, Toronto, in conjunction with Disney Enterprises, Inc. Random House and the colophon are registered trademarks of Penguin Random House LLC.

rhcbooks.com

ISBN 978-0-7364-4203-9 (hardcover)
ISBN 978-0-7364-4204-6 (paperback)

Printed in the United States of America

10 9 8 7 6 5 4 3 2

The Junior Novelization

Adapted by Steve Behling

Random House New York

Prologue

"Listen, Tommaso—do we really need to fish near the island?"

Giacomo studied the old map spread out on a table in the cabin of the small fishing boat. It was night, the sky dark as could be. As the boat made its way out to sea, the tiny coastal town of Portorosso grew smaller and smaller.

"Eh, you worry too much," Tommaso replied, steering them farther into the night. He was much older than Giacomo, and much less prone to concern than the younger man. Aside from the men's voices and pop music playing from their portable gramophone, it was quiet on the water.

Giacomo peered closer at the illustrated map of the Ligurian Sea and western Italy. He noted the ghastly drawings of sea monsters and other horrifying beasts. There was a fearsome kraken, with its deadly tentacles and cold, unfeeling eyes. He pointed at a spot on the map labeled ISOLA DEL MARE that showed a sea serpent tearing right through the hull of an old ship as a siren watched from an outcropping of rocks.

"I dunno," Giacomo said, uncertain. "What if the old stories are true?"

"Oh, come on, Giacomo!" Tommaso scoffed. "You really believe in sea monsters?"

Giacomo shrugged. "Too many strange things have been seen in these waters. . . ." His voice trailed off.

Tommaso wrinkled his brow. "They're all just stories. Tall tales to keep us away from a great fishing spot," the older man insisted.

"But, Tommaso—"

"We're fine. Non preoccupare ti, Giacomo," Tommaso interrupted.

Then the older fisherman cut the engine and the boat began to drift, until at last it came to a stop in the dark water. Ready to start fishing, Tommaso took the pop record off the gramophone and replaced it with an opera record.

"Ah, that's more like it," Tommaso said. He loved listening to opera—the soaring arias, the intricate orchestrations. To him, that was the only kind of music for an evening on the water.

Their boat approached a buoy bobbing in the water with a fishing net attached.

But they weren't the only ones nearing the buoy.

Unnoticed by either man, something was moving through the water—silent and quick.

A fin broke the water's surface, but only for a moment, and then it went back under.

Tommaso continued listening to his beloved opera, unaware of the shadowy arm that reached from the water on the other side of their fishing boat, slicing the rope from the buoy that hung from its hull. The arm took the buoy and disappeared beneath the sea.

As the men focused on the net before them, the mysterious creature grabbed even more items from the boat: a wrench, a drinking glass—even a deck of playing cards.

Giacomo thought he heard something, and turned his head. He could have sworn he saw a sea monster in the shadows, peeking over the water's surface! And it was reaching for the gramophone!

"AHHHHH!" Giacomo shouted. "What is *that*?"

"Oh! Per mille sardine," Tommaso said dismissively.

Then the shadowy figure dove back into the water and swam right into the fishermen's line. Whatever it was, it was becoming tangled.

The fishermen took notice and began to pull the line in.

"Tira, tira!" Tomasso urged.

The boat tipped to one side, and suddenly, a sea monster breached the surface, eyes glowing, as both Giacomo and Tommaso screamed.

The fishing line was cut and the fishermen stumbled backward, knocking the gramophone off the boat and into the dark water.

Shaking, Giacomo reached for a harpoon and threw it toward the water's surface.

"You missed!" Tommaso said. "Let's go—before it comes back for us!"

"I *told* you they were real!" Giacomo insisted.

"Oh, what a monster," Tommaso said, adrift in a sea of fear. "Horrifying . . ."

They sat in silence, watching the gramophone slowly sink into the sea.

Chapter One

"Aaaaaaaahhhh!"

The scream didn't come from a couple of frightened fishermen. It came from the ocean depths. Specifically, from the mouth of twelve-year-old sea monster Luca Paguro.

Luca floated in front of an undersea barn, its doors wide open. Nothing was inside.

His family's goatfish, which were supposed to be in there, were swimming all over the place, eating everything in sight.

"Fish out of the barn!" Luca exclaimed. "Fish out of the barn!"

One of the goatfish bleated.

Luca shouted, "Caterina! Wait!"

But Caterina was already off. Luca followed her, swimming right past another farmer feeding some crabs.

"Good morning, Mr. Branzino—" Luca said hurriedly.

"Ah!" Mr. Branzino shouted, startled by the interruption. "Hi, Luca."

"—and also, I'm sorry," Luca said, struggling with the goatfish. "How's Mrs. Branzino?"

The goatfish kept swimming and Luca left without waiting for an answer. He passed another farmer, Mrs. Gamberetto.

"Excuse me, ah, ma'am?" Luca asked politely. "Have you, by—"

"Yes," Mrs. Gamberetto replied sternly. Then she turned her head, giving Luca an excellent look at the goatfish nibbling on the back of it.

Luca let out a nervous laugh as he quickly collected his goatfish.

But another one had gotten away—it was Giuseppe. Luca saw the fish moving along a hill, heading toward the ocean surface.

"Giuseppe! Get back here!" Luca cried.

He threw himself at the goatfish, but Giuseppe wriggled free. Luca wasn't going to give up that easily. He kept grabbing, and at last, he got a solid grip.

"You wanna run off like your buddy Enrico?" Luca asked. "Because I've got news for you. He's either dead, or he's . . . out there somewhere. Seeing the world . . ."

Luca's voice trailed off, as he imagined what it would be like to go out there somewhere and see the world.

Snapping out of his reverie, Luca said, "But he's probably dead!"

Rejoining the flock, Luca looked at all the goatfish before him and took a quick head count.

"Whew," he said. "Okay. That's everyone."

Then he noticed one of them had a slight grin on its face.

"Monalisa? Why are you smiling?" he asked.

Monalisa just stared as a smaller fish swam out of her mouth.

"Anyone else in there?" Luca asked.

And then a few *more* fish escaped.

Luca was so distracted by Monalisa that it took him a moment to realize that Giuseppe was breaking from the herd once again.

"Giuseppe," Luca said, exasperated. "What did we just talk about. Giuseppe."

But the goatfish kept going.

"All right," Luca said, mustering some enthusiasm. "Let's head out!"

At last, Luca managed to move the flock along the landscape of farms and silos. His neighbors were already out in the fields, tending to their land.

"Hi, Mr. Gamberetto!" Luca shouted. He hoped that Mrs. Gamberetto hadn't told her husband about the goatfish trying to take a bite out of her head.

"Good morning!" Mr. Gamberetto replied with a smile.

Whew!

"Good morning, Mrs. Aragosta!" Luca said as he continued.

"Hey, Luca," she replied.

"Good morning, Luca!" Mrs. Merluzzo said.

"Morning!" Mr. Merluzzo added.

Luca smiled and gave a big wave. "Good morning!"

The young sea monster swam over to the corral on his family's farm and gathered his flock, herding them toward the pasture. When they arrived at the pasture entrance, he stopped the goatfish and peered inside.

"Okay, all clear," he announced, and the fish swam in. "Let me know if you need anything. . . . Anyone?" The goatfish looked up at Luca with blank stares. "No? Okay!"

Then Luca swam over to a rock and sat down. He blew a bubble and watched it drift away for a moment before turning his gaze to one of the goatfish. It was poking at something.

"Giuseppe," Luca said, and he swam over to see what had caught the goatfish's interest. He didn't know it was the alarm clock from the fishermen's boat. To the young sea monster, it just looked like a mysterious round object. The clock began to ring, and Luca panicked until it stopped.

"Whoa," he said. Then his eyes drifted toward the surface of the water. Bright rays of light shone down, illuminating the farm.

Returning his attention to the seabed, Luca looked around some more. A rectangle with strange markings floated in the distance. It was one of the fishermen's playing cards! Luca picked it up, amazed and a bit giddy.

Luca paced around, spotting a shiny wrench in the distance. But before he could swim to it, a rumbling sound, and a shadow moved across the water above.

Luca gasped in horror. "Land monsters!" he screamed. "Everybody under the rock!"

Luca quickly gathered his charges to a small cave. They hid there, waiting for the land monsters to leave. Luca watched in silence as the shadow moved on. For a moment, he wondered what it would be like to pop his head above the surface and see what was really going on up in the land monsters' world.

"Luca!"

The young sea monster jerked his head toward the sound of his mother's voice.

"Lunch is ready!"

"Be right there!" Luca said, and he hid the strange objects near a rock. Then he picked up his crook and herded the goatfish homeward.

"Come on," he said. "We gotta get back."

"You're two minutes late!" said Daniela, Luca's mom. She was waiting for him. "Was there a boat? Did you hide?"

"Yes, Mom," Luca said, sounding as though he'd had a *lot* of practice saying it.

"Because if they catch even a glimpse of you . . . You think they come around to meet new friends? Huh? Make small talk? No. They're here to do murders. So I'm just making sure you know," Daniela said without taking a breath.

"Thanks . . . Mom," Luca said.

Daniela continued her reprimands as they swam inside the house.

"When I was a kid, we'd go weeks without seeing a boat," she said. "And let me tell you, they did not have motors! Just a sweaty land monster with a paddle!"

Luca saw his grandma sitting at the kitchen table. Daniela went to prepare lunch.

"Hi, Grandma," Luca said.

"Hey, Bubble," Grandma answered.

Meanwhile, Luca's dad, Lorenzo, was busy with his prized show crabs. He was cleaning a speckled specimen. "Luca!" he said. "Look at Pinchy-Pessa. She's molting. Oh, it's magnificent! Now, here's a champion show crab if ever I saw one. . . ."

Luca looked at the crab and did his best to sound interested. "Oh, nice." Then he looked at the crab's eye stalks, and right away the creature opened her claws, assuming an attack position!

"Whoa, whoa, whoa!" Lorenzo warned. "Don't look her in the eyes!"

"Sorry," Luca said.

"But don't apologize!" Lorenzo added. "She can sense weakness."

The crab pinched Luca.

"Ow!" he said as Luca's mom pulled the crab from his ear and guided him over to the table.

"Come eat, Luca," she said. "We'd better beat those Branzinos at the crab show this year. Everyone thinks Bianca Branzino's so great, with her prize-winning crabs and amazing dolphin impression. Please! Anyone can do that!"

Luca looked up as his mom did an incredibly accurate imitation of Bianca Branzino's imitation of a dolphin: "*AAAAHEHEHEHEHE!* Right?"

"I don't know why dolphins even sound like that. You know? Why don't they just talk?" Lorenzo asked.

While Daniela and Lorenzo pondered the Branzinos and dolphins, Grandma noticed that Luca was remarkably quiet.

"Luca," Grandma said. "What's on your mind?"

"I—I," Luca stammered. "Well, I was just wondering. Where do boats come from?"

His dad had just taken a bite of his meal. He spat it across the table. His mom gasped.

"The land monster town," Grandma explained. "Just above the surface. I beat a guy at cards there once."

Now it was Luca's turn to gasp.

Both Daniela and Lorenzo were making "Stop!" gestures at Grandma, who either didn't see them or saw them but didn't care.

"Mom! What are you doing?" Daniela asked.

"He's old enough to hear about it," Grandma said with a shrug.

"You've been to the surface?" Luca said in amazement. "And . . . and done the change?"

"Nope! Nope! The end! Shut it down!" Daniela exclaimed.

"I was just curious—"

"Yeah, well, the curious fish gets caught!" Daniela said. "We do not talk, think, discuss, contemplate, or go *anywhere* near the surface! Got it?"

Luca wanted desperately to hear more of Grandma's stories of the land monster town, but he knew there would be no convincing his mom. "Yes, Mom."

"Here," Daniela said, handing Luca a snack. "Now let's get back to work."

Sensing her son's disappointment, Daniela continued, "Hey. Look me in the eye. You know I love you, right?"

"I know, Mom," Luca said, and he left the house, thinking of the world above.

Chapter Two

Luca swam back to the fields, his herding crook in hand, and picked up the shiny wrench he had spotted earlier. He held it in both hands and sighed. Then he noticed something shining in the distance. Swimming toward it, Luca saw a drinking glass.

He picked up the glass and brought it to his face. Turning it around, he looked through the bottom, which magnified everything in the distance.

Then he gasped when he saw something else! Swimming as fast as he could, Luca finally reached it. It was a wooden box with a large metal horn sticking out of the top. This was what land monsters called a gramophone, although Luca didn't know it.

As he got closer to the gramophone, Luca was unaware that something was watching him.

Something wearing a diving suit and carrying a harpoon.

A diver!

The diver was only a few feet away when Luca suddenly turned around, saw the figure, and screamed.

He swam away from the diver, slammed into a rock, and dropped his herding crook.

"Boo," the diver said, taking off his helmet. Luca was shocked to see that underneath, it was just another sea monster—a kid who looked to be around his age. "It's fine," the sea monster said. "I'm not human."

"Oh!" Luca said, laughing nervously. "Thank goodness."

"Here, hold this," the other boy said, handing the harpoon to Luca.

"Uh . . . ," Luca said, uncomfortable about holding the weapon. He watched as the other boy squirmed out of the diving suit and began to pick up the human items from the seafloor, including the gramophone. "Do you . . . live around here?"

"Down here? No, no, no, no, no," said the boy. "I just came for my stuff."

Luca watched as the boy picked up Luca's herding crook and swam off.

"Hey! Wait! That's mine!" Luca said, swimming after him. "Sir? You forgot your harpoon, and—"

"Oh, yeah. Thanks," the boy replied, and took the harpoon. Then he exited the water with his armful of stuff, including Luca's herding crook.

Luca was stunned. He couldn't believe the boy had just left the water!

A second later, the crook broke the surface of the water and hooked Luca. He struggled against it, but he was pulled out of the water and onto the sand!

Luca's hand felt weird out of the water. He looked down as it started to transform. His blue scales were disappearing! Luca screamed and flopped back toward the sea.

"First time?" the boy asked.

"Of course it is!" Luca shouted. "I'm a good kid!"

"Hey," the boy said. "Relax and breathe."

Luca did his best to listen. He breathed, looking around. He saw the bright sky above, and the trees and grass dotting the landscape. He had always wondered about the world above the water. Now he was finally seeing it for himself.

"Well?" the boy asked. "Isn't it great?"

"Uh, no!" Luca answered. "It's bad, and . . . and I'm not supposed to be up here. Good day."

Then Luca raced back into the water.

The boy noticed that Luca had forgotten his herding crook. He picked it up. A moment later, Luca returned, taking the hook.

"Thank you," he said, and walked away.

He came back one more time.

"Good day," he said politely. "Again."

Then Luca disappeared beneath the water.

Try as he might, Luca couldn't sleep. He just lay in his bed, thinking. He looked over at his grandma.

"Grandma," he whispered. "Did you really go up to the—"

Suddenly, Grandma snored loudly. She wasn't awake. She was fast asleep with her eyes open!

Luca sighed and turned away.

The following morning, Luca was out in the fields bright and early. He had gathered a bunch of rocks and made what he thought was a pretty decent representation of himself.

Turning to the goatfish, Luca said, "Okay, everyone. This is, uh . . . Smuca! Yeah. He's in charge now. Got it?"

The goatfish looked at Smuca, then at Luca, and went about their business.

Luca turned away and swam toward the surface of the water. A few moments later he was just about to break through, but he backed off. He was afraid, unsure of what might happen. After all, the first time he'd gone on land wasn't his fault—it was an accident. This time it would be on purpose!

Summoning his courage, Luca approached the surface again, then backed off again.

"Wow."

The voice startled Luca, who turned around and saw the sea monster from the other day, arms full of stuff, staring at him.

"That was hard to watch," the boy said. Then he handed some of the stuff in his arms to Luca. "Here. C'mon."

The boy left the water. Luca took a deep breath, held it, and went right after him.

At the surface, Luca watched in disbelief as the boy transformed from his sea monster form into a land monster! He looked so different. Now he had brown, curly stuff on top of his head. Hair, maybe? The boy flipped the hair, and water went all over.

Luca took a step onto the beach and dropped everything he had been carrying. He tried to shake the water from himself like the boy had done.

And then he transformed.

Luca was mystified. He was a land monster! The only sign of his previous form were his seaweed shorts! He turned around, looking for his tail, only to see that it, too, was gone.

"Wait," Luca said. "It feels like it's . . . still there."

"Yeah, that's called phantom tail," the boy said. "You'll get used to it."

Luca picked himself up off the beach, and fell right over.

"Right," the boy said. "Walking. Don't worry—you're in luck. I basically invented it."

With effort, Luca rose on his legs and managed to stand up without falling down.

"To start, stack everything, one on top of the other. Like a pile of rocks," the boy said, watching Luca adjust his body with a loud grunt. "Great. I mean, fine, whatever. Now, walking is just like swimming. But without fins. Or a tail. And also, there's no water. Otherwise, it's like the exact same thing. Give it a try."

Luca looked at the boy and took a step forward. He fell onto the sand.

"That's not it," the boy said. "Try it again."

Luca tried it again, and fell onto the sand again.

"Oh! Try to lead with your head," the boy advised. "No. More belly."

Luca had no idea what that meant, but he kept on trying.

"That's . . . that's lying on the ground," the boy said. "How about this. Just take a step without even thinking about it."

"I don't know how to not think about something!" Luca said, completely out of his element.

"Okay, okay," the boy replied. "Watch."

The boy stood up and walked over to Luca. "Point your feet where you want to go. Okay? And then just catch yourself before you fall."

Luca gulped and pointed his feet forward. Then he got up and took a step.

This time he didn't fall over.

Then he took another step.

And another.

"Good . . . good . . . yes. Yes!" the boy shouted.

Luca was walking! "I'm getting it!" he yelled.

"Not bad, kid," the boy said. He reached out a hand to introduce himself. "Alberto Scorfano."

"Luca Paguro," he said. With great confusion, he took Alberto's hand, and his new friend pumped it up and down. He didn't know that was called a handshake.

"Piacere, Girolamo Trombetta," Alberto said. Noting Luca's confusion, he continued. "It's a human thing. I'm kind of an expert."

"What does it mean?" Luca asked, eager to learn. "The thing you just said?"

Alberto looked at Luca, then suddenly changed the subject, "C'mon, I'll show you some more stuff!"

The two boys carried Alberto's stuff up a hill until they arrived at the base of a small abandoned-looking tower. An old weather-beaten ladder rested against its side.

"Mother of pearl!" Luca said. "You live up here?"

"Yeah. Me and my dad. He's not even here a whole lot, so I pretty much just do whatever I want."

"Isn't it dangerous?"

"Yeah," Alberto said. "It's the best. Everything good is above the surface."

Then Alberto's eyes widened as he prepared to illustrate for Luca all the good things above the surface.

AIR!

"Air!" Alberto yelled. Luca took a deep breath, inhaling as deeply as he could. But he accidentally inhaled a bug and Alberto had to help him cough it out.

GRAVITY!

Luca had no idea what gravity was, so Alberto demonstrated. He scrambled to the top of the tower and yelled, "Gravity! Also known as—"

He jumped off the tower and into a tree . . . then he fell out of the tree.

"—FALLIIIIIING!"

THE SKY!

Alberto pointed. "The sky . . . clouds . . . sun . . ."

Luca noticed the brilliant yellow orb that floated in the blue sky.

"Whoa, don't look at it!" Alberto said, covering Luca's eyes. Then he chuckled, uncovering them. "Just kidding. Definitely look at it."

Luca screamed, temporarily blinded by the bright yellow orb. He did not look at it again.

"And then . . . there's human stuff," said Alberto, rubbing his hands together. He climbed the ladder to his home and Luca followed.

Inside, Luca couldn't believe what he saw. A big mess! There was human stuff *everywhere.* Old, rusty things littered the place.

"As you can see, I've been collecting for a long time,"

Alberto boasted. "So ask me anything." Luca immediately focused on the gramophone.

"Ah, yes, that's the Magic Singing Lady Machine," Alberto said. "It's broken, unfortunately."

Looking at the machine, Luca saw a handle, and began to turn it. Suddenly, the gramophone came to life with a woman's beautiful singing voice.

"Whoa!" Alberto said. "You unbroke it!"

As they listened to the music, Luca's attention drifted over to a big poster hanging on Alberto's wall. On it was a large, boxy thing on two wheels. "What's that?" Luca asked.

"Oh, that's just the greatest thing that humans ever made," Alberto said. "The Vespa. You just sit on it, and it takes you anywhere you want to go. In the whole stinkin' world."

" 'Vespa is freedom,' " Luca read from the poster. Then he slowly looked around the room at the incredible collection Alberto had been gathering. "Are you gonna make one? I think you have all the parts."

Alberto's eyes widened as he, too, gazed at the objects that surrounded them. There was a wheel over there, and something else that could be a wheel, and a rocking chair that could work as a seat.

"I do have the parts," Alberto said, stunned. "I *am* gonna make one! You wanna help?"

"Me?" Luca said. "Yeah! Wait. No, I can't. I gotta go home."

"Right this second?" Alberto asked.

"Yeah. If my parents found out I was up here . . . ," Luca mused. "Oof. It would be bad. So thank you, but goodbye." He looked at the Vespa poster sadly. "Forever."

Then he looked at the poster again.

One Hour Later

"Okay, but now I really do have to go," Luca said.

In just an hour, they had managed to build the basic framework for their Vespa scooter.

"Okay," Alberto said.

Another Forty-Five Minutes Later

"Seriously, I have to go, like, now," Luca said, looking at the Vespa, which they'd found wheels for. "Like, right now."

"Uh-huh," Alberto answered.

And Two Hours After That

"It's even better than the picture!" Luca cried. He looked at their one-hundred-percent homemade Vespa, full of excitement.

"Yeah, it is," Alberto agreed.

At last, Luca said, "Oh, gotta run!" and he bolted for the ladder.

"See ya tomorrow!" Alberto called as Luca waved goodbye and disappeared.

Chapter Three

"Luca? Where have you been?" his mom called.

Luca rushed into the house, hurrying toward the table for dinner. Don't say surface, *he thought.* Don't say surface.

"Surface," Luca said, quickly covering his mouth with his hand.

"What did you just say?" Daniela said, her eyes narrowing at her son.

"What's wrong with your foot?" his dad shouted.

Luca looked down at his foot and saw that somehow it was still human! "Ahhhhh!" he shouted.

This would all have been very troubling if it hadn't just been Luca's imagination.

In reality, he was standing in the doorway of his home while his mom waited for him to answer her question.

"Luca?" Daniela said.

"Uh, I . . ."

"Gonna tell us where you were?" she prodded.

All Luca could manage to say was "I . . . uh . . ."

"It's my fault," Grandma said, jumping in. "I sent him to look for sea cucumbers."

Luca looked at his Grandma, relieved. "Right. Sorry, Grandma, I couldn't find 'em."

"Mom," Daniela said with a huff. "His life is maybe a little more important than your snacks."

Grandma shrugged.

"Thank you," Luca whispered to his grandma.

Dinner came and went with no further questions about his whereabouts, and Luca went to bed right afterward. Once again, he found himself unable to sleep. But this time, he was ridiculously happy, thinking about his day—and the day to come.

"Whoa! How'd you get it down here?" Luca asked. He stared at Alberto, who was standing on top of a hill, holding on to their homemade Vespa.

"I rode it down," Alberto said.

Luca stared at him.

"I didn't," Alberto admitted. "I pushed it out the back window. Took a while to put back together, but it's fine now. You ready to ride it?"

Alberto pointed at an incredibly steep hill, at the bottom of which was a small wooden ramp. It looked exactly like the kind of thing Luca would not like to do.

"Oh. Well, thank you, but no thank you," Luca said. "I mean, I just think maybe I would die."

"Okay, I'll ride it," Alberto said. "You hold the ramp."

"Uhhh . . ."

The next thing Luca knew, he was at the bottom of the hill and under the ramp, holding it up.

"Sir? Maybe we should sleep on it?" Luca yelled.

But Alberto wasn't listening. He jumped onto the Vespa and screamed, "Whatever you do, *do not move!*"

"I'm not the guy you want for this!" Luca moaned. "I'm more of an idea man! I—"

"Take me, Gravity!" Alberto shouted, and he kicked off from the top of the hill, thundering toward destiny.

But on its way, the Vespa hit a rock. The scooter changed course, and Luca moved the ramp accordingly. Suddenly, the Vespa broke in half. Alberto was now riding the front half like a unicycle, struggling to keep it upright and trying to brake with his bare feet.

"This is normal!" Alberto shouted. "Stay focused!"

As the half scooter careened down the hill, it continued to lose pieces—pieces that sailed right by Luca, who managed to duck behind the ramp to avoid getting hit. He peeked over the top and saw Alberto being hurled off the lone wheel. The boy was now somersaulting end over end, rolling right for him!

"Don't move, don't move, don't move!" Alberto ordered, and Luca ducked under the ramp. Alberto rolled over the top, splashing into the water just beyond and hitting a bunch of rocks.

"He's dead," Luca said to no one. "I've killed him!"

But Alberto wasn't dead, not by a long shot. He thrust his fists in the air and shouted, *"WHOOO!!!!"* And he laughed!

"Wait, that was *good*?" Luca said, confused.

"Did you see the height I got?" Alberto chuckled as he got out of the water. "Hey, nice ramping." He slapped Luca on the back. "Come on, let's build another one!"

Luca looked at his new friend and was surprised to find that he was no longer afraid. He smiled and nodded.

Soon Luca and Alberto were spending every day together, exploring Isola del Mare and working on their second Vespa.

Alberto took the opportunity to show Luca more of the cool human stuff he had found. There was a sword and a buoy with a rope. Alberto swung the buoy around like some kind of weapon and managed to hit himself in the head with it.

Another time, Alberto gave Luca some human clothes to replace his seaweed shorts and they danced to music from the gramophone.

Eventually, their second homemade Vespa was ready. With Luca once again holding the ramp, Alberto set off down the hill. But a seagull attacked Luca and he had to abandon the ramp! Another Vespa was destroyed.

While Luca was having fun with Alberto above the surface, Luca's rock creation, Smuca, kept a watchful eye on the goatfish. But because Smuca was made of rocks, that meant absolutely no watching was happening. And Luca's mom noticed.

Both Daniela and Lorenzo were stunned to discover that their son wasn't tending to the goatfish, and that he had, in fact, constructed a rock replica of himself instead. They looked all around the fields where Luca normally would have been.

That was when they discovered his stash of stuff.

Human stuff.

A few days later, Daniela and Lorenzo observed Luca in the fields, piling rocks to build his rock structure yet again. They couldn't believe it. Where was he sneaking off to?

Daniela shuddered to think.

Back above the surface, Luca had no idea his parents had discovered the truth about Smuca. He was having too much fun with Alberto.

Alberto took off at a full sprint for the edge of the land

and jumped. He sailed through the air, landing with a big splash in the water below.

Luca was about to follow, when he stopped and stepped back. He took a deep breath, determined to make a run for it, just like his friend. He ran for the edge, but at the last second, he came to a halt. Or he *tried* to stop. Instead, he stumbled, slipping right off and belly-flopping into the water with a loud *SLAP!*

After their swim, Luca and Alberto were watching the open water and saw a fisherman scream at a passing speedboat. The craft was creating a big wake, roiling the water and disturbing the fish.

"What's wrong with you, stupido?" the fisherman yelled.

Alberto liked the sound of that phrase, so he decided to practice it. "What's wrong with you, stupido?"

At the end of another fun day, the two friends ended up in a cove. Luca picked up a couple of sea snails and styled his hair with their slime so it looked like Alberto's.

Everything was perfect.

"Look, we gotta ride together," Alberto said. He was at the top of the hill with another homemade Vespa, but this time Luca was up there with him. "If you don't sit on the back and hold on to the front, the whole thing falls apart."

"Oh . . . and who's holding the ramp?" Luca asked.

"The turtle," Alberto said, as if that was entirely obvious.

He pointed at the ramp, which was slowly shuffling away. "C'mon, he's faster than he looks."

Luca wasn't sure about that, but he really wanted to try it. So he said, "Oh, okay. Here we go!"

But he didn't move.

"You, uh . . . you coming?" Alberto asked.

"Nope," Luca answered flatly. "I can't do it. Never in a million years."

"Hey, hey, hey. I know your problem. You got a Bruno in your head."

"A Bruno?" Luca gasped. He didn't like the idea of having anything in his head, except maybe his brain, which was kind of necessary.

"Yeah," Alberto continued. "I get one, too, sometimes. *'Alberto, you can't. Alberto, you're gonna die. Alberto, don't put that in your mouth.'* Luca, it's simple: Don't listen to stupid Bruno."

Luca pondered this for a moment, then said, "Why is his name Bruno?"

"I don't care. It doesn't matter. Call him whatever you want. Shut him up. Say, 'Silenzio, Bruno!' "

"Silenzio, Bruno," Luca said weakly.

"Louder!" Alberto ordered.

"Silenzio, Bruno!" Luca said, sounding more confident.

They kept repeating this until at last Alberto asked, "Can you still hear him?"

"Nope," Luca replied. "Just you!"

Then Alberto picked Luca up and put him on the back of the Vespa. "Good. Now hang on!"

Alberto checked his image in the rearview mirror, and with a strong kick, he sent them rolling down the hill. "ANDIAMOOOOOO!"

Holding tight to Alberto, Luca could feel the Vespa bouncing on the ground, hitting every rock along the way. It didn't help that Alberto wasn't exactly an expert at steering. The Vespa was wobbling all over the place! Which meant that it wasn't headed for the ramp.

"Whoooooooo!" Alberto shouted joyfully.

"AHHHHHHH!" Luca screamed in fear. He closed his eyes tight, then made the mistake of opening them just for a second—as the Vespa began to fall apart! Luca held on to Alberto even more tightly.

"Silenzio, Bruno. Silenzio, Bruno. Silenzio, Bruno. Silenzio, BRUNOOOOOO!" Luca yelled, just as Alberto managed to steer the Vespa back on course. Amazingly, it hit the ramp. For a brief, shining moment, they were in the sky, flying!

Then, for another brief moment, they were falling toward the water! Specifically, toward one razor-sharp rock!

The boys screamed as they fell. At the last possible second, Luca had a thought. He let go, shoving Alberto away from him, and the boys splashed down on either side of the rock, missing it entirely.

Alberto bobbed up and down in the water, shooting a fist into the air in victory. Luca cheered, and so did Alberto.

"Yes! We're alive! I can't believe it! Yes!" Luca roared.

"Yeah! Take that, Bruno!" Alberto hollered.

"What are all those tiny lights?" Luca asked, gazing at the lights dotting the evening sky. The boys were on the roof of Alberto's hideout, near a warming campfire.

"Anchovies," Alberto said. "They go there to sleep."

"Really?" Luca asked.

"Yeah," Alberto said. "And the big fish protects them." He pointed at the moon. "I touched it once. I dunno; felt like a fish."

Luca couldn't believe it. Was there anything Alberto *hadn't* done?

"Wow. Your life is so much cooler than mine," Luca mused. "I never go anywhere. I just dream about it."

"You came up here!" Alberto reminded his friend.

"Thanks to you," Luca replied, turning his attention to the sky once more. "Otherwise, I never would have seen any of this."

After a while, Luca looked at the lights across the water. "Have you ever gone to the human town?"

"Yeah," Alberto said. "Uh, no," he amended. "But my dad told me all about it. So I'm pretty much an expert."

"Your dad sounds so cool."

Something about Alberto's demeanor suggested he didn't feel so lucky. "Yeah," he answered.

There was silence, and then Alberto said, "Hey, you remember that time we almost hit that rock?"

Luca laughed.

"And we flew through the air, and I was like, 'YEAAAAHHH!' And you were like, 'NOOOOOO!' "

Luca kept laughing, holding his sides.

"Wouldn't it be amazing to have a real Vespa?" Luca said, and the words hung in the air.

"Yeah. That's the dream."

"Yeah . . . ," Luca replied, and he fell asleep. This was, of course, a very bad thing, because it meant he wouldn't be going home. Which meant his parents, who were already so, so worried about him, would be even *more* worried.

When he woke with a start, he shouted, "Oh no, I fell asleep!" and woke up Alberto, too.

Then Luca ran for the steps, heading for home.

Somehow, Luca had managed to make it all the way home and sneak into his room without waking anyone up. Grandma was sleeping, snoring as usual. Now all he had to do was slip into bed, and no one would know.

Except that his mom was standing in the doorway, arms folded, staring at him.

Chapter Four

Luca's mom sat him down at the dining room table. Luca held on to his tail, nervous, as he saw the various human items he had collected spread out on the table.

"Uhhh . . . ," was all Luca could think to say.

His dad was there, too, but it was his mom Luca was worried about. She was sitting on the other side of the room, and he couldn't tell what was going on in her head. Was she going to scream at him? Punish him? Scream at him *and* punish him?

"Daniela, do we really need to go through with this?" Lorenzo said, breaking the silence.

"With . . . what?" Luca asked.

"Son, you're in big trouble," Lorenzo said. "You need to promise us that you'll never sneak off to the surface again."

"I'm really sorry," Luca said, and he meant it. "But you

know . . . it's not that dangerous up there! Maybe I could show you—"

"I told you," Daniela said to her husband angrily. "Our son has a death wish!"

"But, Mom! We're always careful—"

Instantly, Luca realized his mistake, and covered his mouth.

"We?" Daniela and Lorenzo said in unison.

"Me and my friend . . . Alberto," Luca began. "But it's okay! He's one of us."

"Ah, yes. There's usually a bad influence," said a voice.

Luca turned to see a sea monster emerge from the shadows. The monster looked just like his dad, except his skin was transparent, his eyes were milky, and he was generally kind of scary to look at.

"Good thing you sent for me when you did," the sea monster said.

"Luca, this is my brother. Your Uncle Ugo," Dad said.

"Thanks for coming on such short notice," Daniela said.

"Of course," Uncle Ugo replied. "Hello, Luca. Nice to—"

But before he could finish his sentence, Uncle Ugo froze and made weird gasping sounds, like he was having an attack.

"Oh, he's okay," Dad said. "Just punch his heart. Just a little tap."

Luca was horrified, but he obeyed anyway. He flicked Uncle Ugo. A second later, Ugo gasped as his heart started up again.

"Thanks for that," Uncle Ugo coughed. "Too much oxygen up here. Not like the deep. As you'll learn."

"What?" Luca asked. He didn't like where this was going.

"Sure, there's no sunlight, but there's nothing to see anyway . . . or do. It's just you and your thoughts. And all the whale carcass you can eat. Little bits of it just float into your mouth—you can't stop it, you can't see it." Uncle Ugo rambled on. "C'mon, no time to waste!"

"Mom? What does he mean?"

"You're going to stay with Uncle Ugo for the rest of the season," Daniela answered.

"No!" Luca said, panicked. "I can't!"

"*Two* seasons, then. Want to go for three?"

"Why are you doing this?" Luca asked.

"The world is a very dangerous place, Luca!" Daniela replied. "And if I have to send you to the bottom of the ocean to keep you safe, so be it."

"You don't know what it's like up there!" Luca said, his voice rising.

"I know you! And I know what's best for you," Mom said. "It's *done*."

Luca glared at his mom.

"Hey, look me in the eye," she said. "You know I love you, right?"

But Luca wouldn't give his mom the satisfaction of a response. Instead, he whirled around and headed to his bedroom.

Daniela wanted to say something that would make everything better, but she had no idea what that would be.

Luca fumed in his room. He looked at his bedroom window, then at his bedroom door.

In that moment, he knew what he had to do.

Luca left through the window, unaware that his supposedly sleeping Grandma was watching him leave.

"This is so unfair!" Luca said, raging. He had headed right for Alberto's place and was now pacing the floor as Alberto listened. "They're sending me to the deep! To live with my weird see-through uncle! What do I do?"

"I dunno," Alberto said. "Stay?"

"Up here?" Luca asked. "They'll come looking for me."

"Okay," Alberto replied, knowing his friend was right. "That may be true. But . . . will they come looking for you over there?"

Alberto looked toward the town of Portorosso.

"No way," Luca said. "That's crazy!"

But Alberto was undeterred. "I mean, that place must be full of Vespas. There's gotta be one for us."

Luca thought for a moment, staring at Portorosso. "A real Vespa . . . ," he said, his voice trailing off. "Could we even survive over there?"

"You and me? We can do anything!" Alberto insisted. "We'd swim right over to Vespatown, track down Signor Vespa—"

"Wait, do you really think there's a Signor Vespa?" Luca asked.

"Makes sense, right?"

"Yes. Continue."

"And we say, 'Signor Vespa! Build us one of these!' " Then Alberto pulled out the diagram he had made of their custom Vespa.

To Luca's eyes, the Vespa looked amazing. It had all sorts of cool features. But the best feature had to be the extra-long seat, where both he and Alberto could sit.

"Whoa. This is the greatest drawing I've ever seen," Luca said.

"Yeah, I know!" Alberto replied. "Luca, think about it. Every day, we'll ride someplace new. And every night, we'll sleep under the fish. No one to tell us what to do. Just you and me out there. Free."

Free.

Luca liked the sound of that.

A while later, Luca and Alberto ran for the water. As Alberto reached the edge, he jumped off, screaming, "Take me, Gravity!" Then he did a backflip off the cliff and splashed into the sea.

Luca was right behind, and he hesitated, just for a moment. He looked at the town of Portorosso, and he could hear all the reasons he shouldn't go echoing in his head. Then, at last, Luca said, "Silenzio, Bruno."

And with a loud "Wooo-hoooo!" he jumped, joining Alberto in the water.

They had changed back into their sea monster forms when they hit the water. Now they started to swim toward the town. Luca just wanted to be in Portorosso already. Unfortunately, he was moving so quickly that he failed to notice the big rock he was about to swim into!

Lucky for him, Alberto pulled him out of the water. In the air, for the briefest moment, they transformed into land monsters. Then they hit the water again and changed back into sea monsters. They continued swimming.

Thrilled at how alive he felt, Luca kept jumping out of the water, enjoying the quick transformation into land monster before returning to his original form. He and Alberto leapt in and out of the water all the way to Portorosso.

Chapter Five

"Whoa," Luca said as he broke the surface near a buoy. In front of him was Portorosso—a beautiful human town. Luca had never seen anything like it.

Almost immediately, they were spotted by a girl fishing in a boat.

She gasped.

Luca gasped.

Alberto gasped.

The girl shouted, "Papá! What's that?"

Immediately, Luca and Alberto ducked out of view.

"How do we get in?" Luca asked. He spotted something—a sunken boat just beneath them.

They swam under the boat and put it over their heads. Then they started toward the shore, emerging from the water. They kept walking with the boat so they could change into their land forms beneath it. Passing by an older whistling fisherman, Luca was surprised they'd made it this far.

Eventually, he and Alberto were able to climb over some rocks and ditch the boat. Then they started toward town.

"This'll be a breeze," Alberto said confidently. "Just don't get wet."

Luca felt a surge of panic. He watched as Alberto took a stride toward town, and a couple of fishermen turned the corner. They carried fishing hooks and dead fish.

Luca gasped. "Actually, this town seems a little crowded." He turned, ready to leave, when Alberto stopped him.

"Hey," Alberto said. "Silenzio, Bruno."

Bruno was still screaming, so Alberto had to drag Luca along, past the fishermen.

Alberto looked at the men, and, wanting to be friendly, remembered something he'd overheard before. "What's wrong with you, stupido?" he said.

The fishermen stared at Alberto.

"Huh. It worked!" Luca said in disbelief. They had made it past the fishermen and were now approaching a corner.

"See?" Alberto said. "You just gotta follow my lead."

They turned the corner and saw the busy town in all its glory. There were people everywhere, talking, smiling, laughing. Some kids were kicking a ball around, and others were eating something big and green with a red middle. Luca would later learn that the land monsters called it watermelon, and it was delicious.

Some people were playing a game with little rectangles

that looked very much like the objects Luca had found in the field while herding goatfish.

Luca and Alberto were enthralled by the bustling town and all the people. They hardly noticed when two older women walked near them, each holding something in their hands.

"Classic human town," Alberto said. "Pretty cool, right?" The women came closer, and he whispered to Luca, "Hey. You do it now. Just say the thing."

Luca watched nervously as the two women ate something. The something turned out to be gelato, which, as it turned out, was like ice cream, which, as it turned out, was delicious.

"Madams?" Luca said to the women. "What's wrong with you, stupido?"

The women gasped, then glared at Luca. Whatever he'd just uttered, it wasn't good.

So not good, in fact, that one of the women hit Alberto with her umbrella, and the other smacked Luca with her bag.

The women stormed off, leaving the boys with gelato cones on top of their heads. The gelato melted down their faces.

"Maybe I said it wrong?" Luca asked. The gelato dripped into their mouths, and their faces lit up at the taste of the new treat!

As he enjoyed the gelato, Luca's eyes drifted around town, where he noticed something quite disturbing. There were numerous statues and frescoes—paintings—featuring the same person: a man with a mustache, who was slaying what could only be described as sea monsters.

Luca gulped uncomfortably. He grabbed Alberto's arm and started to drag him back to the water. "Alberto, this is too dangerous!" he said. "Let's get out of here!"

"And—and go where?" Alberto asked.

Before Luca could say anything else, there was a rumbling sound. It reminded him of the motorboats he had heard back in the sea, but this was different. Then he saw a Vespa! A real Vespa!

Someone was riding it, someone with lots of sea slime in his hair. At least, Luca thought that was what made his hair so tall.

"It's Signor Vespa!" Alberto gasped.

The adults seemed annoyed to see the older boy who had just ridden in on the Vespa. "Mannaggia. Here we go." said one person, rolling their eyes.

"Buongiorno a tutti!" the boy, named Ercole, replied in greeting.

A priest came running out of a nearby church, hands clamped over his ears.

"Oh, mamma mia! Please, no more revving," the priest cried, shaking his head.

"Ciao, ciao! Ha, ha!" Ercole said, clearly enjoying the attention. "Beep, beep! Pride of Portorosso coming through!"

Ercole passed the two women Luca had just insulted. "Ciao, belle," he said to them. "You're making me blush!"

"Disgaziato!" exclaimed one of the women, annoyed.

"Blech," replied the other.

A crowd of kids cheered nervously as Ercole rode around the plaza. They seemed fearful of the boy.

Ercole showed off with a couple of tricks, like riding his Vespa with no hands. This impressed Luca to no end. He wondered how such a thing was even possible.

Two other kids around Ercole's age approached him, carrying a long sandwich. Eventually, Ercole stopped the Vespa and dismounted.

"Now!" Ercole announced. "Who wants to watch me eat a big sandwich?" He walked to a table at a nearby café as his friends set up his lunch.

"There it is!" Alberto said. "That's how we're gonna see the world!"

He and Luca walked toward the Vespa just as a soccer ball landed in front of them.

"Hey! Little help?" said the kid who had kicked the ball.

Luca kicked the soccer ball back but misjudged his strength. The ball sailed across the piazza—and smashed right into the Vespa!

A collective gasp went up from the crowd, and Ercole looked like someone had just destroyed his life.

"La mia bambina!" he shouted, rushing over to the Vespa.

As the vehicle tipped over from the impact of the soccer ball, one of Ercole's sandwich-holding friends slid under it, cushioning the fall.

"Oh, mamma mia!" Ercole said, examining the Vespa. "Talk to Ercole. Are you hurt?"

"Well, my head kinda hurts," said the kid who had stopped the Vespa from falling.

"Not you, Ciccio," Ercole said. "Out of the way! If there is so much as a scratch . . ." Unconcerned for his friend, Ercole examined the Vespa. Once he was satisfied that there was no damage, he turned to face the crowd. "Someone got lucky today. Who got lucky?"

The kid who had kicked the soccer ball to Alberto and Luca pointed at the pair.

Ercole walked over to them, looking them up and down with barely disguised disgust. "Out-of-towners, eh? Let me welcome you. Benvenuti a Portorosso! Ciccio?"

Ercole untied his sweater and handed it to the still-recovering Ciccio. "I am delighted to meet you, number one. And number two, I love your stylish clothes. Where did you get them? A dead body? I'm kidding!"

Ciccio chuckled, and so did Ercole's other friend.

"Uhh . . . look, Signor Vespa—" Alberto started.

"Signor Vespa? Ha, ha, ha. This guy is funny. I am Ercole Visconti, five-time winner of the Portorosso Cup."

"The Portorosso what?" Alberto asked.

"The Portorosso Cup! Per mille sardine—how do you think I paid for my beautiful Vespa?"

While Ercole spoke, Luca couldn't take his eyes off the scooter. It was possibly the most beautiful thing he had ever seen in his life.

As if sensing this, Ercole shouted, "You! Stop looking. She's too beautiful for you."

Luca tried to speak, but only stammered, backing away.

Ercole sneered. "The little guy can't even get a word out. And he smells like behind the pescheria."

"Hey, my friend smells amazing!" Alberto said, getting right in Ercole's face.

"Sorry, sorry! I'll make it up to him," Ercole said, but his tone suggested that he didn't really want to help. "Ciccio. Guido."

At that moment, Ercole's friends picked Alberto up while Ercole grabbed Luca, and they walked the boys over to a fountain. The two friends struggled, afraid of what was about to happen.

Things didn't get any better when they actually saw the fountain, which featured a statue of the mustached man killing yet another sea monster.

"Ah, just a little bath!" Ercole said in a mocking tone. "It's funny, eh?"

Ercole shoved Luca's face toward the water, and the boy panicked.

"No, no, no, no, no!" he shouted. As he got closer and closer, little droplets hit his face, causing patches of it to turn green—revealing his true sea monster self!

Chapter Six

But before Ercole could really give Luca a bath, he was distracted by someone shouting, "Hey! Ercole, basta!"

Ercole turned to see a girl on a bike pulling a cart full of fresh fish. She barreled through and Ercole jumped out of the way, releasing Luca. Luca quickly dried his face and hid behind the girl's fish cart.

"Oh, look who's here," Ercole said. "Spewlia's here. Wow. That's how you're training for the race?" He pointed at the girl's fish-cart bicycle.

"Si certo! Your reign of terror is coming to an end!" said the girl, whose name was most certainly *not* Spewlia.

"You mean, like a year ago?" Ercole said. "When you quit in the middle of the race? Because you couldn't stop throwing up?

"I didn't quit," the girl said. "They made me stop."

Ercole smirked. "I think that is worse. Now go away. I'm having fun with my new friends."

"They're coming with me," the girl replied. She turned to Luca and Alberto. "Hop on. I could use the extra weight."

She faced Ercole, stuck out her tongue, and unleashed an epic raspberry. *"THHHPPPPBBBBBBTTT!"*

She began to pedal as the boys hopped onto the fish cart.

"Fine! Go start a club! For losers!" Ercole shouted at her. "Ha! I'm kidding!"

Meanwhile, the adults were ignoring Ercole completely. There was something else going on.

"Another sighting, Maggiore," the fisherman Giacomo said. "In the harbor this time."

"I know," Maggiore replied, holding up a poster. "We're setting a reward. Someone's gonna win a nice prize . . . ."

Ercole snatched the poster. "Me! I win the prizes! Ciccio, get your daddy's harpoon! We're gonna catch a sea monster!"

Luca and Alberto exchanged nervous looks as the girl pedaled away. Even with their added weight, the girl was going very fast. She turned a corner and groaned loudly.

"Sto imbecille!" she said. "Thinks he can be a jerk, cuz he keeps winning the race, which he shouldn't even get to do anymore, cuz he's too old and too much of a *jerk*!"

The boys stared at her.

"You know we underdogs have to look out for each other, right?" she said.

They just stared, wondering what she was talking about.

"What's under the dogs?" Alberto asked, genuinely curious.

"*Under*dogs," the girl explained. "You know. Kids who are different, dressed weird . . ." She raised her arm, revealing a glistening, sweaty armpit. "Or are a little sweatier than average."

She had stopped pedaling, and the boys jumped off. Luca stood behind Alberto, not sure what to do next.

"Too much? Too much," the girl said. "So, are you in town for the race?"

Luca and Alberto had no idea what she meant.

"The Portorosso Cup?" she continued, but they still didn't say anything.

"Well, good talk," said the girl. "I gotta deliver these. Always be training, you know."

But as she walked away, Luca realized something. He grabbed Alberto.

"We should ask her about the Portorosso Cup race. That's how the loud, scary human said he got his Vespa."

Alberto understood.

"Hey, uh, Spewlia," Alberto said tentatively.

The girl whose name was most definitely *not* Spewlia whirled around from her first delivery and gave Alberto a look that stopped him where he stood.

"*Giulia.* My name is Giulia," she said. Then she turned around and set out for her next delivery.

"Uh . . . when you . . . race . . . in a cup," Alberto began, not wanting to upset Giulia any more than he already had, "what do you get?"

Giulia reached into her pocket and pulled out a handful of shiny coins. "Soldi," she said. "Prize money."

"Oh," Alberto said, not impressed.

"Okay . . . ," Giulia replied, shaking her head.

Giulia walked ahead, and the boys followed. At once, Alberto and Luca started arguing with each other.

"No, no! Keep going!" Luca said.

"What? Why?"

"Ask her about the prize money!"

"But that stuff is useless!"

"Maybe it becomes a Vespa!"

"How does that become a Vespa?"

"Just ask her!"

"Fine, fine, fine!"

"Hello, again," Alberto said, returning to Giulia's side.

"Ciao."

"Can we turn the money into something else?" he asked. "Like, something like—"

They rounded a corner and passed a garage. Parked right in front was a bright, shiny, new Vespa scooter.

"That!" Luca exclaimed, pointing at it.

"*Pffft.* No," Giulia said. "But it could get you *that.*"

Giulia pointed to a very rusty, very used Vespa standing right next to the bright, shiny, new one. To Luca, it still looked like the most amazing thing in the world. He gasped, imagining himself and Alberto as a cascade of gold coins showered down around them, and then a moment later, taking the wheel of their very own Vespa, which they had paid for with all those gold coins.

"It's so beautiful," Luca said quietly.

"Yes," Alberto agreed. "We need it."

Giulia hopped back on her bike and began to pedal as the boys walked alongside.

"Great! So we'll just win the race!" Alberto said.

At those words, Giulia hit the brakes. "You'll have to beat Ercole," she said.

"Okay, so we'll beat Ercole."

Now Giulia hopped off her bike and walked right up to the boys, glaring at Luca. "Huh. Really?" she began. "Thinks he'll beat Ercole, this guy. First of all, get in line! Every summer, that jerk makes my life miserable. So no one's taking him down, unless it's me!"

Alberto realized he had chosen his words quite poorly. Before he could apologize, Giulia said, "Second, this isn't any old race. It's an epic, grueling traditional Italian triathlon: swimming, cycling, and eating pasta."

The boys were speechless.

"So you'd need a teammate," Giulia added.

"Well, we'll figure it out," Alberto said. "Thanks, human girl."

They watched as Giulia pedaled her bicycle and cart

away. Alberto started to walk in the opposite direction, and then Luca suddenly stopped his friend.

"Hey, hey, wait, Alberto," he said. "What if we join her team?"

Alberto frowned. He wasn't used to other people stopping him and suggesting ideas. Ideas were kind of his thing. But he thought for a moment, then said, "Better idea."

He turned and yelled to Giulia, "Hey! Congratulations! You're joining our team!"

Giulia laughed and called back, "I race alone."

Then Giulia's cart got stuck and she couldn't pedal. The boys ran over to her, helping to push her bicycle and cart forward.

"But we could be under the dogs, too," Luca said as he pushed the cart with great effort.

"Hey, it's okay, Luca," Alberto said, playing it cool. "She'd rather do the whole race alone again. Maybe this time she won't throw up as much."

"Uh, hang on," Giulia said. She fixed her gaze on the boys, like she was staring into their souls. "You wanna be on my team, eh?"

The next thing Luca knew, he found himself sitting on Giulia's bicycle.

"Let's see what you got," she said.

Chapter Seven

Luca sat on Giulia's bicycle, which she had disconnected from the fish cart. He was nervous yet thrilled to be sitting on an actual bicycle.

"Whoa!" he said as he put his foot on a pedal and pushed it down. The bicycle moved forward slowly, catching him by surprise. He looked around and saw people walking around the piazza, staring at him.

Feeling self-conscious, Luca gulped and tried to ride. He wobbled a bit, and glanced at his feet to see how he was doing. He fell right over. And unlike in water, it hurt when he hit the ground.

"All right, try jumping on it!" Alberto suggested.

Luca tried, and fell.

"No, no, no, you gotta show it you're the boss!"

Luca was unable to show the bicycle that he was the boss, and fell. Again.

"It can tell you're afraid," Alberto said with authority. "Wrestle it into submission!"

"Santa Mozzarella," Giulia muttered, having had quite enough of this. "Eyes up!" she said to Luca.

"Huh?" Luca said.

"Looking down is what's making you fall," she said.

That made sense to him, so he started to pedal the bicycle. This time he looked forward, not down. To his great surprise, he was doing it! He was riding a bicycle! And not falling!

"Oh yeah, I was gonna say that, too. About looking down," Alberto said, knowing he totally wasn't going to say that. "So, can we be on the team?"

Giulia looked annoyed. "Aspetta! Can you dodge obstacles? What if an old lady crosses your path?"

Then Giulia imitated one and got in Luca's way. He barely managed to avoid her.

"Can you withstand passive-aggressive verbal assaults?" Giulia shouted. "Nice bike, number one, and number two—I was kidding, your bike is a disgrace! Ha, ha, ha, ha, ha!"

Luca cowered, but he kept riding.

"And finally," Giulia said, leaning some wooden planks on some barrels to make a very tight obstacle course, "can you handle the course's fiendishly difficult terrain?"

"Silenzio, Bruno," Luca said as he maneuvered the

bicycle through the course. He wobbled all the way—but he was doing it!

Well, he was until he looked down to check his feet. That was the end of that—he went right over. Luca stood and picked up the bicycle. He was going to try it again.

"Stop," Giulia said to Luca. Then she turned to face Alberto. "What about you? Can you swim, at least?"

"Yeah, I'm amazing—" Alberto said, and Luca gave him a sharp jab with his elbow. "—ly bad at swimming."

"You can't swim, you can barely ride a bike . . . siete un disastro!" Giulia moaned. "I mean, where are you even from?"

"Wouldn't you like to know?" Alberto said. "We're runaways!"

"Runaways? I dunno, ragazzi," Giulia said, thinking.

"Please!" Luca begged. "My family was going to send me somewhere horrible, away from everything I love. But if we win this race, well, we can be free!"

Giulia looked at Luca and her face began to soften. She faced Alberto, who said, "My life's great. I'm just helping him out."

"Just give me one more chance," Luca pleaded. "I know I can do it this time."

He was about to ride when Giulia stopped him. "No. You guys want it just as bad as I do. You have the hunger. That's the most important thing."

"I'm definitely hungry," Alberto said.

"Perfetto!" Giulia exclaimed. "You eat, you bike, and I swim." She indicated Alberto, Luca, and herself, respectively.

Luca couldn't believe it. This might actually work! He looked at Alberto, who smiled.

"Underdogs?" Giulia said, suggesting a team name.

"Underdogs!" Luca and Alberto cheered.

"Now we just need money for the entry fee," Giulia said. "From my dad."

The boys followed Giulia through town and all the way to her house. They had never been to a land monster's house before, so it was at once exciting and utterly terrifying. Inside, Luca saw a heavily tattooed man with one arm making dinner in the kitchen. He was singing loudly.

"All right. Just let me do the talking," Giulia said. "And act casual. He doesn't do well with fear."

Neither do I, Luca thought.

"Hey, Papá!" Giulia called. "I brought some friends for dinner. Is there enough for four?"

The huge man with one arm turned around, holding a massive cleaver in his hand. "Hmmm?" he said.

Luca felt like he was going to pass out.

"Whoa," Alberto said.

The man glared at the boys, looking them up and down. Then, without a word, he nodded, turning around to continue making dinner. Giulia gave Luca and Alberto a thumbs-up.

A few minutes later, the boys found themselves seated at a table. Luca was terrified. Alberto looked around the small room and spotted harpoons hanging on a wall.

"What do you think he kills with those?" he whispered to Luca.

The big tattooed man, whose name was Massimo, chopped off the head of a fish with his cleaver. He overheard Alberto. "Anything that swims," he said.

Luca laughed nervously.

"Visto the giornale today?" Massimo asked, handing the local newspaper to the boys. The headline said MOSTRO AVVISTATO ALL'ISOLA and featured a blurry photo of a sea monster with its tail peeking just above the water.

"Ugh, that photo's a fake, Papá," she said. "Everyone in Portorosso pretends to believe in sea monsters."

"Well, I'm not pretending," Massimo said. He tore the photograph out of the newspaper and stuck it to the wall with a knife. Then he went back to cooking. Giulia helped.

Luca and Alberto got a good look at the wall, and saw it was completely covered with similar photos of sea monsters, all torn from newspapers. He was drinking a glass of water, and immediately did a spit take. In that moment, Luca wanted nothing more than to crawl back into the sea.

The water hit Alberto on half of his face, which promptly transformed into its sea monster form!

Luca grabbed Alberto and pushed him to the floor under the table.

"Huh?" Giulia said as she and her father turned around.

Luca quickly wiped Alberto's face with his shirt. He was glad that neither Giulia nor her father could see them, or knew what had just happened. But there was another pair of eyes watching them.

It was a cat.

The cat had seen it all. The cat knew their secret.

With a nervous laugh, Luca returned to his seat, and so did Alberto. They pretended that nothing out of the ordinary was going on. Giulia shrugged and continued cooking with her father.

Luca noticed that the cat was still staring at him.

Then Massimo said, "Dinner's ready. Trenette al pesto. Mangiamo." The man plopped onto his chair, and it felt like the whole room shook.

Staring at the pasta on his plate, Luca wondered how the land monsters ate. He saw there was a small stick with pointy things at one end, which he later learned was a fork. He picked it up, and Alberto did the same. Then both boys glanced at Giulia and her father to see what they would do.

This was a fine plan, except Giulia and her father were waiting for their guests to start first.

Luca smiled and laughed awkwardly as Alberto took the lead. Alberto set his fork down and reached right into the pasta with his hands, shoving it into his mouth.

Massimo shot Alberto a look.

Then Luca picked up some pasta with his hands, too.

"Uhhh . . . ," Giulia started to say.

The boys ate with gusto, ramming handfuls of pasta into their mouths as Massimo furrowed his brow. They didn't seem to notice him as they kept on eating.

At last, Massimo asked, "Where did you boys say you were from?"

Luca didn't know what to say, and felt even more uncomfortable when he noticed the cat was still staring at him. It was now sitting on Massimo's shoulder, watching.

"They're uh, classmates!" Giulia said, thinking fast. "From Genova. Luca and ahhhh . . ."

"Alberto," Luca said softly.

". . . Ahhhhlberto."

"And what brings you to Portorosso?" Massimo asked.

"Oh, uh, funny you should ask," Giulia replied. "They came for the race."

"The race?"

"Yeah," Giulia said. "Uh, you know what? Don't worry about it."

"Don't worry about it?" Massimo said, wondering what his daughter didn't want him to worry about.

"Mmm-hmm, don't worry about it."

Of course, this made Massimo feel he should definitely worry about it, so he set down his glass, sighed heavily, and said, "Giulietta? A word?"

"I don't want you doing the race again," Massimo said, gesturing for Giulia to speak with him privately. "You get so upset—"

"Papá, per favore," Giulia protested. "I have a team now." She gave Massimo her most determined look.

Her father sighed again. He knew that when his daughter set her mind to something, there would be no changing it. "There's also the entry fee," Massimo said. "Money's tight. . . ."

"I'll work double shifts at the pescheria," Giulia said quickly. "Whatever you need—"

"I can't sell what I don't have," Massimo insisted. "What I need is more fish in my net. Mi dispiace, Giulietta."

"Um, excuse me?" Luca said, interrupting their conversation. "We could help."

"You know fish?" Massimo asked.

"Oh, we know *lots* of fish," Alberto chimed in.

Massimo thought about it, and saw the look on his daughter's face. There was no possible way he could say no to her, not this time.

"You want to work, I'll put you to work," Massimo said.

"Really?" Luca replied, excited, pumping a fist in the air.

"Oh, grazie, Papá!" Giulia said.

At this point, the cat had settled on the table, glaring at Luca. To say this was unsettling would be an understatement.

Giulia said, "Machiavelli! *Pssssst!*"

Machiavelli yowled. He bared his teeth, hissed, and showed his claws.

"Don't you . . . No!" Giulia shouted. But Machiavelli pounced on Luca!

"I'm so sorry about the cat," Giulia said as she and the boys hurried out of the house and into her backyard. "I don't know what got into him."

"It's fine," Luca said. "We're gonna head back to, uh . . ."

"Oh, do you guys need a place to stay?" Giulia asked. She looked up at a tree, indicating a wooden platform positioned in its branches.

Luca smiled at Alberto, and the boys gratefully accepted Giulia's offer. They climbed up the tree and onto the platform, with Giulia following them.

There were three books laid out on the platform, and Giulia quickly scooped them up. "Sorry, this is my—"

"Your hideout," Alberto said.

"Heh," Giulia chuckled. "Yeah. My hideout. Buonanotte, boys."

Giulia descended from the hideout with the books, and walked over to her bedroom window. She climbed through the window, then fell inside, books flying.

"Slipped!" she said, popping up. "See you in the morning!"

As Giulia disappeared from view, Luca let out a big sigh. "That was close."

"I know!" Alberto said. "Like, how big was that dad human? That guy kills things, for sure."

"I thought we were gonna die like a hundred times," Luca said, realizing it might have been even more than that.

"Hey, relax," Alberto said, trying to reassure his friend. "We're incredible at this human-ing stuff."

"Yeah," Luca said, thinking about it. "You're right!"

They sat there quietly for a moment.

"Did you see me on the bike?" Luca said. "Giulia said, 'Look up,' and then all of a sudden, I was riding it!"

Alberto nodded, but he didn't seem impressed. "Yeah, yeah, yeah. Our Vespa's gonna be even better than a bike, though. Because the moment we get it, we're outta here."

"I can't wait," Luca said with a smile. He rolled onto his back and looked up at the bright lights sparkling in the night sky.

Chapter Eight

Daniela rose from the water and went out into the night in her land monster form, determined to find her wayward son. Lorenzo followed close behind. They looked around for any sign of land monster activity. The coast appeared to be clear.

"How could my mother tell him about this town of bloodthirsty lunatics?" Daniela said.

"I still can't believe he would do this," Lorenzo replied. "It's not like him."

"Just keep your guard up," she said. "There's gonna be land monsters everywhere—"

Then she turned around and saw a land monster standing right behind her! She went on the attack. First, she knocked the land monster onto the sandy beach. Then she started to smack the creature in the face!

"Not today, land monster!" she shouted with all the fury she could summon.

"Daniela!" the land monster protested. "Wait, what? Ow! Ow! It's me!"

Daniela instantly realized her error—she hadn't recognized her own husband in his land monster form! "Ah, you scared the scales off me!" she said, rubbing her husband's cheek.

"Gosh, you're strong," Lorenzo said. "Owww."

"I'm sorry," Daniela said. "I'm just a little on edge."

"No, I needed that. It really woke me up." Then Lorenzo took a look at himself and at his wife. "Wow! We look horrifying."

Daniela examined her hair, which, by land monster standards, was quite nice-looking. "Ugh," she complained. "Gross. Come on, let's find our son."

But before they could begin their search, they saw an actual land monster approaching this time! Thinking fast, they dove behind some rocks.

At this rate, how would they ever be reunited with Luca?

The following morning, Luca opened his eyes and saw a bird sitting on a tree branch. Water droplets dripped from the leaves, indicating a recent rain. Luca smiled, unaware that the rain had gotten all over the platform, causing him to transform into a sea monster.

His expression changed when he turned over and saw Alberto, who was also in his sea monster form.

"Oh no. Oh no! Alberto, wake up!" Luca said urgently.

"Huh? What?" Alberto said. "Ahhh! The sky's leaking!"

The boys heard a loud *SLAM* and stared at each other. Looking down at Giulia's windows, they saw that the shutters were open. Giulia was in the window, cupping her hands to her mouth. She proceeded to imitate the sound of a very loud, very obnoxious trumpet.

Not knowing what else to do, the boys vacated the platform, trying to escape Giulia's view. They disappeared behind the tree just as the back door opened and Massimo leaned out. He was holding a bunch of harpoons in his hand.

Luca gulped as he and Alberto dried off before anyone could see them.

Except someone *had* seen them.

It was

that

cat.

Machiavelli was sitting there atop the fence, watching them. He had seen everything! Luca knew that the cat knew what they were, which made him super anxious.

"Oh, there you are!"

It was Giulia, and luckily, both Luca and Alberto had changed to their land monster forms. "Uh, buongiorno," Luca said.

"All right, ragazzi," Massimo said to the kids. "You

want that entry fee, you gotta earn it. Giulia, you make the deliveries."

Giulia grabbed a list from Massimo and hopped onto her fish-cart bicycle. She pedaled away. "I'm on it!" she called. "Already makin' 'em! Ciao!"

"You two are coming with me," Massimo insisted.

Luca gave Alberto a nervous look. But Alberto didn't seem to be nervous—or if he was, he didn't show it. Instead, he seemed fascinated by the multiple knives that Massimo had.

"Which knife do I get? Huh? Huh?" Alberto asked.

"You don't," Massimo said.

The water was calm as Massimo took his fishing boat out of the harbor.

"Buongiorno, Massimo!" an old fisherman said from a passing boat. "You'll keep an eye out for those sea monsters, right? We're all counting on you!"

Massimo grasped the harpoon, showing it off. "Don't worry, Tommaso. I've got my eyes peeled. . . . They won't get away."

Luca laughed again, more anxious than ever. He and Alberto were sitting in the back of the fishing boat. Even Alberto looked worried now.

The wake from the other boat hit Massimo's, and the

small fishing boat began to rock with the waves. Luca lost his balance and very nearly fell overboard.

As the boys struggled to avoid falling into the water, Massimo seemed not to notice. He just hummed an opera and kept his eyes fixed on the sea.

Another wave rocked the boat, and Luca was thrown to the other side.

"Hey, this isn't a joyride," Massimo said. "Make yourselves useful."

When they had boarded the boat, Massimo explained what he wanted the boys to do. They reached over and started to pull up some fishing nets. Luca couldn't help noticing that Machiavelli, who had unfortunately come with them, was watching his every move. The cat hissed at him.

Alberto's attention drifted to Massimo, fascinated by the man's missing arm.

"A sea monster ate it," Massimo said.

Alberto looked horrified, and Massimo laughed. "Ma, no. This is how I came into the world."

Then Massimo pulled a fish onto the ship. "Not a great catch today."

"It might be because we're over a haunted fish graveyard," Luca suggested.

Massimo looked puzzled as Alberto jumped in. "We know it's not haunted," he explained. "The fish think it's haunted."

Now Massimo looked *really* puzzled.

"This time of day, most fish will be *riiiiiight* about there," Alberto said, pointing somewhere in the distance.

"Hmmm," Massimo said, wondering if the boy had any clue what he was talking about.

A while later, Giulia rode her fish-cart bicycle down to the marina. She pedaled furiously, trying to make the trip in record time. When she pulled into the marina, Giulia skidded to a halt and checked her time.

She shot her fist into the air and cheered, "New personal best!"

Looking up, she watched as her father and the boys returned from their fishing expedition. She did a double take when she saw the massive amount of fish they had caught.

"Santa Pecorino," she said quietly, in awe.

"Your friends do know fish," her father said, and he slapped Alberto on the back, nearly knocking him into the water!

"Benissimo!" Giulia said. "Let's go sign up!"

Chapter Nine

Daniela and Lorenzo found some land monster clothes hanging on a line to dry. Now that they were dressed to blend in, they approached the town of Portorosso.

"Okay, okay. What's our plan. Think, Daniela!" she said.

"Hey," Lorenzo said. "Everything's always on you. I want to step up."

"Uh . . . you sure?" Daniela said skeptically.

"Oh, yeah," he said, spying something. "I got this one."

Lorenzo saw a kid sitting all by himself on the seawall, eating gelato.

"Oh, hello there, young man," Lorenzo said. "You're not fooling anyone."

The kid stared back.

"Did you really think you could get away with this?" Lorenzo continued.

"Lorenzo," Daniela said through gritted teeth. "Uh-uh . . . Lorenzo . . ."

"You thought we wouldn't find you," Lorenzo said, and now the kid was looking pretty nervous. "Well, it's time for us to go home."

"I don't think—" Daniela said, but by then, Lorenzo had already pushed the kid right into the water. He was about to jump in after him when Daniela yanked him back.

The kid was still a kid. He hadn't turned into a sea monster, let alone their son, Luca.

And the kid was crying.

"Let that be a lesson to you!" Lorenzo said.

"Go, go, go, go!" Daniela ordered. "Run, before its mother gets here!"

So they ran away.

"It turns out I don't got this," Lorenzo observed.

"No, but I do. I'll know my son when I—"

Daniella gasped as they ran into the piazza.

It was brimming with kids.

"—see him," she said, finishing her thought. "Aw, sharks."

Giulia, Luca, and Alberto left the marina and headed straight for the piazza so they could stand in line and submit their entry to join the Portorosso Cup.

There was a line of kids waiting to do the exact same thing, but it did nothing to dampen Luca's excitement.

Something else was waiting to do that.

Standing in the piazza was a woman dressed in an elaborate costume. Giulia looked at her and grabbed a box of pasta from a nearby display. She held the box so it covered the woman's face. On the back of the box was a picture of an elaborately dressed, mustachioed man—a man who looked very familiar to Luca. Giulia then lowered the box of pasta, revealing a mustache on the woman, just like the one sported by the man on the pasta box.

With a flourish and much bravado, she said, "Fellow Portorossans! It is I! Giorgio Giorgioni! Slayer of sea monsters and beloved purveyor of pasta!"

Luca was terrified. He gasped. That was the face on the pasta box! That was who the woman was pretending to be—the guy on the fountains and paintings they had seen! "Slayer of sea monsters?" he said.

"*Pffft.* I could take him," Alberto replied.

"Ahh, that's just Signora Marsigliese," Giulia explained. "She works for Pasta Giorgio Giorgioni, the sponsor for the race." Watching the woman, Giulia sighed. "This is gonna take forever."

"The finest pasta in Liguria. At a price every family can afford!"

"Get to the rules!" Giulia yelled.

"Enthusiasm!" Signora Marsigliese said. "Love to see it! To follow in my footsteps and win my famous race, your team must be the first to brave the treacherous waters of the bay! Devour a mystery bowl of my delicious pasta! And ride to the top of Mount Portorosso—and back!"

"That all sounds pretty hard," Luca said, sounding dejected.

"Yeah," Alberto said. "Hard to *lose*! We're going to win!"

Giulia grabbed both Luca and Alberto by their heads and turned them so they faced all the kids who had lined up to enter the race. "I love your confidence," she said. "But the competition looks brutal this year."

She gestured at a very tall girl with broad shoulders who was stretching.

"Carlotta once outswam an angry dolphin!" Giulia said.

Then there was another kid, with a really, really long tongue, who was eating.

"Danilo's fork skills are insane. But the biggest obstacle, as always, will be—"

Right on cue, Ercole arrived in the piazza, with Ciccio and Guido right behind him. Guido was holding a sandwich for Ercole, as he usually did.

"Champion coming through!" Ercole announced. "Ciao, ciao! Ay!"

The crowd parted, the kids shrinking away from the bully.

"Ercole," Giulia groaned.

Ercole walked to the front and put down his entry fee.

"Aren't you a little old?" asked Signora Marsigliese.

"Signora!" Ercole exclaimed in mock outrage. "I'm sixteen!"

"You said that last year."

"But this year it's true!"

"You might want to save your money, ragazzi," Ercole said to the crowd. "This year, Ercole's gonna make it six in a row."

Suddenly, he noticed Giulia, Luca, and Alberto standing there, and he smiled. "I don't believe it! Spewlia, you teamed up with these vagrants?"

"Ignore him," Giulia said.

"Oh, I wish for you that you could. Unfortunately," Ercole said with a sniff, "I'm afraid your friends still need to pay the Out-of-Town Weirdo Tax." Then he snapped his fingers, and Ciccio took the money right out of Giulia's hand and gave it to Ercole.

"Hey!" Giulia shouted. "Ercole, you have to give it back!"

"Ercole doesn't have to do anything," he explained. "He's the Portorosso Cup champion, number one, and number two, his life is amazing and everyone loves him."

"They don't love you! They're afraid of you!"

Ercole turned to the crowed, leaning in close. "Raise your hand if you love me."

Terrified, everyone in the crowd raised their hand.

"See? Everyone," Ercole said. Then he turned to Alberto, "Even you. Boop."

Ercole tapped Alberto on the nose. But Alberto had heard enough. "Oh, that's it. Come on, Luca," he said.

"Hey!" Ercole laughed. "The vagrants want to fight? Wow, che bello!"

Luca wasn't so sure about this. Actually, he was sure that this was a terrible idea. "Alberto . . . ?" he protested.

"Silenzio, Bruno," Alberto said. "Remember, this is for our Vespa!"

But before any fighting could begin, Giulia wedged herself between the two groups of boys. "Stop," she said.

Luca was afraid, but he raised his fists anyway, to protect himself.

"A Vespa?" Ercole said. "*Pfft.* Ha, ha, ha! Trash like you can't ride Vespas!"

"Ercole, you're just afraid we're gonna put an end to your evil empire of injustice," Giulia said, but frowned as she realized Ercole was saying her exact words at the same time she said them. It was a comeback she had used many times before.

"Got anything new?" Ercole asked.

"Yeah!" Giulia said, her mind racing. "Here's a new one! You look like a . . . umm . . . a . . . uhhh . . . a catfish!"

The crowd looked at one another, not quite sure what that meant. Ercole definitely didn't know.

So Luca jumped in. "Uh, they're bottom-feeders, and they also have two sad little whiskers," he said.

A collective gasp rose up from the crowd. Then there was a loud *"OOOOOOHHH."*

And then the laughter started.

Even Guido snickered a little, but he covered his mouth just as soon as he started.

Ercole was angry. So angry, in fact, that he removed the salami from the sandwich and smacked Guido with it.

"Listen Piccoletto," Ercole said, turning his attention to Luca. "I eat kids like you for breakfast. I dunk them in my cioccolata and *gnam*! Finiti!"

Ercole made a slicing motion across his neck. Then, he leaned in and put an arm around Luca, which was way more intimidating than anything else he had done yet.

"So, here," he said, returning Giulia's money. "Sign up. I'll make it my mission to destroy you."

Luca felt his entire body go numb.

"Ha, ha, ha!" Ercole said, joking with the crowd. "It's gonna be some race, huh? Sorry, no autographs today!"

As he walked away, he pointed to a boy who still had his hand raised from earlier.

"You. You can put your hand down."

Luca wanted to disappear. Then he felt another arm around him. Except this time, it was Giulia!

"Ha, ha! Luca! Bravo, we did it!" she said.

Luca wasn't sure what they had done, exactly, but at least now he could breathe again. Giulia pulled him away, with Alberto right behind them. They approached a table, and Giulia placed her money down.

"Giulia Marcovaldo!" the girl said proudly.

"Ciao, Giulia," Signora Marsigliese said. "Team of one?"

"Not today!" she said, nudging Luca.

"Luca Paguro!" he said.

"Alberto Scorfano," said Alberto.

Alberto sounded a little reluctant to sign up as a team, but the others were too excited to notice.

Chapter Ten

"Okay, ragazzi!" Giulia asked as she set a big bowl of rigatoni in front of Alberto. "We have one week to train. Pronti, ai posti, via!"

Ready, set, go!

"I got this," Alberto said. He was just about to dig in when Luca walked over from Giulia's kitchen, setting down another bowl of pasta. It was spaghetti.

"Wait, what?" Alberto exclaimed.

Then came another plate, of fusilli.

"Every year, they change the pasta," Giulia said. "You have to be ready for anything! Could be cannelloni, penne, fusilli, trofie, even *lasagne*!"

Alberto shrugged and tried to play it off like it was all no big deal. He was about to shovel the pasta into his mouth when Giulia stopped him and handed him a fork.

"Aaaaand, you have to use a forchetta. It's the rule."

"Ugh!" Alberto groaned. "Rules are for . . . rule people!"

But the boy had no other choice than to eat with a fork. On that day, Alberto knew frustration.

Luca wondered exactly how big the hill was that he was on. It seemed that he had been pedaling the bicycle up it for hours. In reality, it was probably a minute. Maybe less.

He turned and saw an old man walk past him carrying a bag of groceries.

How was the man walking faster than he was pedaling?

Luca sighed as Alberto and Giulia walked behind him.

Eventually, impossibly, he reached the top of the hill. He took one look down and saw how steep it was. It was really, *really* steep.

"Holy carp," Luca said. "No, I can't!"

Then Ercole rode by on his bicycle. "I know, I know. Ha, ha, ha! And remember, Piccoletto—"

Ercole repeated the slicing motion across his neck.

"Forza!" Giulia shouted. "Luca, don't let him get in your head. You can do this!"

"Okay," Luca said, taking a deep breath. "Silenzio, Bruno! Here we go!"

Then he pushed off, his bicycle picking up speed. Everything was going great until Bruno decided to start talking in his head, and suddenly, Luca said, "Ahhh! Ahhhh! I can't!"

Hitting the brakes, Luca watched as the front wheel

locked up. He tumbled over the handlebars. The bicycle hit the ground, and so did Luca, and unlike the bicycle, he didn't stop. Luca just kept rolling down the hill until he collided with a pushcart full of flowers.

In that moment, Luca knew he did not like rolling down hills and hitting flower carts.

A little later, the three friends headed down to the shore. It was time to help Giulia practice the swimming part of the race.

Luca and Alberto were in a rowboat, keeping pace with Giulia. Luca tried to ignore the pain in his arms as he rowed. Alberto slowly rowed with the other paddle as they watched Giulia swim toward a buoy.

"I guess that's how humans swim," Luca said.

"Ugh, that's embarrassing," Alberto replied.

In the distance, Ercole, Ciccio, and Guido approached in a small motorboat.

Giulia noticed them instantly, and her eyes went wide as she watched the boat come closer. "Ercole!" she shouted. "Go! Go!"

Alberto and Luca began to row faster. However, apparently Luca was rowing in one direction, and Alberto was rowing in the other, because their rowboat just went around in circles.

"Luca! Faster!" Alberto ordered.

"Why aren't we moving?" Luca asked, exasperated. Ercole's motorboat was even closer now, and drawing nearer every second.

Ercole grinned broadly—it really seemed like he was going to run the boys down!

At the last moment, Guido grabbed the wheel, turning the motorboat away to avoid a collision. The movement created a wave. The wave missed Luca, but it struck Alberto! He immediately turned into a sea monster, so he ducked down into the boat.

Ercole turned to Guido, furious. "Guido?" he said, his anger boiling over.

"I . . . I slipped!" Guido insisted.

"Ciccio! Slap Guido!" Ercole commanded. "Again! Like you mean it!"

Giulia swam over to Ercole, shouting, "Ma sei scemo, Ercole!"

Luca knew he had to hide his friend, and did his best to cover him with a tarp. But all he succeeded in doing was hitting Alberto in the face and knocking him into the water.

"Huh?" Ercole said, looking over at the boat with only Luca sitting in it. "Where did the other one go?"

Suddenly, something broke the surface of the water.

"Huh? Cosa?" Ercole said, distracted for a moment. But before he could do anything, an angry Giulia tipped Ercole's boat over, toppling him.

"Ercole! Che cavolo stavi pensando, eh?" she screamed.

Ercole's sweater fell into the water, and the young man fished around for it. "Sei matta! Giulia! It is wool! It cannot get wet! Ciccio, make it dry. Subito!"

With Ercole distracted by his urgent sweater situation, Luca was able to reach over the side of their boat and pull Alberto aboard.

Unfortunately, Giulia also chose that moment to come aboard. "Luca? Alberto?" she said.

Luca quickly threw the tarp over Alberto—and this time, he didn't knock him into the water.

"Are you okay?" she asked.

Alberto dried off as fast as he could. He transformed back into a land monster before Giulia noticed.

"We're good!" Alberto said. "Good, good, good."

"Well, I think that's enough training for today," Giulia replied.

As the kids began to row home, Ercole finally looked up from his wet sweater.

"Argh! Ciccio! The motor! They are slowly getting away!"

Ciccio fumbled with the motor, failing to start it.

"Giudo! Slap Ciccio!" Ercole shouted. "Per mille sardine—with contempt!"

While Guido reluctantly slapped Ciccio, Ercole watched Giulia, Luca, and Alberto make their getaway.

Almost immediately upon their arrival at the piazza, Daniela thought she saw Luca. She ripped the hat off the boy only to find that it was, in fact, not Luca.

She moaned, disappointed, as she watched a group of kids play soccer. The ball soon rolled over to Daniela, and she looked at it.

"Hey! Over here! Kick it!" a kid said, and Daniela kicked the ball. It was a really good kick—so good that it hit a little girl and knocked her right into the fountain.

"I have an idea!" Daniela said.

Lorenzo called after her, but she ignored him. She walked over to a group of kids and asked, "Can I play, too?"

She started to play with them. She was super competitive. Almost immediately, she stole the ball from one of the kids and hip-checked them into the fountain.

"Oh . . . okay," Lorenzo said, taking a step back. He watched as his wife dominated the game. The kids raced after Daniela, but they were no match for her skills. One by one, she played against them, and one by one, she knocked them all into the fountain!

It took Lorenzo a while to realize what she was doing. Daniela was narrowing the list of suspects by process of elimination! Each time a kid went into the fountain and didn't transform into a sea monster, they knew it wasn't Luca.

"Not our kid," Lorenzo said as another one went in. "Not our kid . . ."

"Let's see Bianca Branzino do that!" Daniela said, then did the dolphin call better than Bianca Branzino ever could. But they still hadn't found Luca.

"Where could he be?" Daniela wondered, catching her breath.

"Well, at least you won!" Lorenzo said, finding the bright side. "I think."

"We just gotta keep looking," Daniela said, determined.

Luca and his friends had just reached the piazza. Luca could have sworn he saw his parents.

Noticing that her friend had stopped, Giulia grabbed him and guided him along with Alberto toward her yard. Luca shook his head, trying to make sense of what he had just seen.

"Good effort, team," she said. "You've earned your pasta tonight."

"Can I please eat with my hands?" Alberto begged.

Chapter Eleven

All through dinner, Luca had been quiet—quieter than usual.

Alberto was thoroughly disappointed that he had to eat dinner with a fork. He was in no danger of earning the title Fork Master, which wasn't even a real title, but he was getting better.

After dinner, Luca and Alberto retired to Giulia's hideout in the tree.

At last, Luca spoke.

"Uh, Alberto?" he said nervously. "I think I might've seen my parents."

"No way," Alberto said. "I told you, they're not coming here."

"But what if they did? They're gonna send me to the deep!"

Alberto shook his head. "Listen, relax. It's never gonna happen."

Suddenly, Giulia appeared. "All right, boys. Pretty good today, but let's talk technique!"

In the yard below, Massimo looked up at the hideout. "Hey, ragazzi!" he said. "I need some help with the nets." He pointed at Alberto. "You! The big strong one. Andiamo."

Alberto didn't want to leave Luca, but realized he had to. "I'll be right back," he said, then ducked off the platform and down the tree. He followed Massimo out of the yard.

Giulia could see that something was off with Luca, so she said, "Hey, we're gonna win. And you'll get your Vespa. Why do you want a Vespa again?"

"Oh," Luca said, pondering the question. "Because it'll be amazing. Every day, me and Alberto are gonna ride someplace new. And every night, we'll sleep under the fish."

He pointed at the bright lights in the dark sky.

Giulia arched an eyebrow. "The . . . fish," she said, playing along. "Heh . . . good."

"How about you? What'll you do when you win?" he asked.

Giulia smiled. "Ohh . . . ho-ho, I'll get up in front of everyone and say, 'I told you I'd win!' "

"Yeah!" Luca cheered, then looked confused. "And then what?"

"Well, that's it," Giulia said. "Look. During school, I live with my mamma in Genova. And every summer, I come here, and everyone thinks I'm just some weird kid who doesn't belong."

"I think I know how you feel," Luca said.

Giulia was relieved to finally have someone to talk to who understood. "Right? That's why we gotta win! The town will cheer our names—Ercole's life will be ruined!"

Luca stared at her.

"Sorry. Too much? My mom says sometimes I'm too much."

"No way!" Luca said. "Not for me."

Giulia laughed as they looked up at the stars together. "You know those aren't fish, right?"

"Of course they are!" Luca insisted. "Alberto told me all about it."

"Come with me," Giulia said.

They left the hideout, and a few minutes later, Giulia had them climbing up onto a rooftop. Then she and Luca began to walk along the rooftops of Portorosso. She jumped effortlessly from one to the other. Luca, afraid at first, followed, surprising himself.

Crossing her neighbors' houses, Giulia eventually took Luca to a rooftop that had a little platform. And on that platform was a long metal tube on three legs.

"This is a telescope," Giulia explained. "Old Man Bernardi lets me use it. It makes far-away things seem close. Look."

She directed Luca to the telescope. He bent and peered through the opening. Inside, he saw a cluster of brilliant lights in the sky, none of which resembled fish in the slightest.

"See any . . . fish?" she asked.

"Then what are all those?" Luca asked.

"Stars," Giulia said. "Like the sun. Giant, raging balls of fire!"

Luca thought for a moment. "So . . . Alberto was wrong?"

"And stars are circled by planets," Giulia continued.

Luca was beyond excited. He stared up at the sky, trying to take it all in. Then Giulia handed him a book called *L'Universo.* It was filled with brilliant pictures of the stars and planets.

Turning back to the telescope, Giulia searched for something in the sky.

"Look," she said, showing Luca. "That's Saturno. It's my favorite."

The planet appeared to have rings around it. Rings!

Luca imagined what it would be like to actually run on those rings.

Later that night, Luca sat in Giulia's room, poring over her schoolbooks. He couldn't believe all the amazing facts they contained!

"And we're all on a big round rock, floating around a star, in the . . . solar system?" Luca asked, paging through one of the books.

"So cool, right?" Giulia said.

"And is there anything beyond the solar system?" he asked.

"Only a galaxy full of solar systems!"

"Then what?"

"A universe full of galaxies!"

Luca laughed. "And THEN what?"

"And then . . . ," Giulia said, "I don't know! But next year in advanced astronomy, I'm gonna use my school's telescope. So maybe I'll find out! That thing's *huge.* I wish I could show it to you."

Luca grinned and stood up. "Just promise you'll tell me everything you see!" he said, and in his excitement, he sounded like Giulia. "Sorry. Too much?"

"Never," Giulia said, and she meant it.

"Hey, Luca!" Alberto said, standing outside the window. "I've been looking everywhere for you."

"Oh, sorry," Luca said, and he noticed that Alberto was glaring at him.

"Just come on, let's go," Alberto said tersely.

Staring at the book in his hands, Luca turned to Giulia. "Could I maybe borrow this? Just for tonight."

Giulia took the book from Luca's hands and picked up a

pen. She scribbled something on the first page and handed it back to him. Staring at the page, Luca saw that she had written something.

Luca

The name was right below the "This book belongs to" line.

"You can have it," Giulia said. "The universe is literally yours!"

"Wow!" Luca said, amazed. "Thank you!"

Alberto popped up once more and said, "Luca!"

"Oh—okay," Luca said, not wanting to leave. He went out the window and joined Alberto.

"Where are we going?" Luca asked.

"Come on, I got something to show you."

Alberto had led Luca out into Portorosso's night streets. His head was still buzzing with wonderment from all the things he had learned from Giulia.

"Hey, you won't believe this!" he said, pointing at the sky. "Those aren't fish!"

"What?" Alberto said.

"Yeah! Giulia explained it to me. They're fires. But like one million times bigger—"

"Uh, no, they're not," Alberto said, cutting off his friend.

Luca didn't know why Alberto was being that way, so

he walked in silence. Alberto was quiet, too. At last, they reached their destination—the mechanic's garage they had visited the other day, the one with their Vespa. They looked in the window and saw the beat-up scooter sitting there, with a little sign that said FOR SALE.

"Soon you'll be ours, sweet Vespa," Alberto said with a sigh. Then he put his drawing up against the window. "Take a look. I thought of every single thing we're gonna need. Also, I added flames."

"That's so cool!" Luca said. Then he started to draw on the window. "And we can bring a telescope, too!"

Alberto stared at Luca's telescope drawing, and then he added some lightning coming out of it.

"No, no, no," Luca said. "You look *through* it."

He erased the lightning, and Alberto looked disappointed.

But Luca continued, "Giulia says there's an even bigger one at her school." That was when it hit him. "Wait! What if we visit her there?"

"Why would you want to do that?"

"It . . . kinda sounds interesting," Luca said.

Alberto wasn't having it. "The whole reason we're getting a Vespa is to live on our own! We don't need school! We don't need anybody!"

"Couldn't we just try it?" Luca asked. "Just for a few days?"

"Luca, sea monsters can't go to school. What do you think is gonna happen when they see your fish face?"

Before Luca could answer, something long and metallic slammed into a nearby sculpture of a sea monster.

It was a harpoon.

Someone had just thrown it.

That someone was Ercole.

Luca Paguro is a cautious but curious sea monster. He works on his family's goatfish farm and is forbidden to go above the surface.

Luca meets Alberto Scorfano, an adventurous sea monster who lives above the surface. Alberto collects items from the human world.

When they're dry, sea monsters look like land monsters! Alberto invites Luca to his hideaway and teaches him all about the human world.

Alberto dreams of owning a real Vespa. For now, he's content with the one they made with Alberto's collection of human items.

Luca and Alberto realize that riding a homemade Vespa is harder than it seems. They try again and again, but each time, it falls apart.

Despite this challenge, Luca and Alberto become good friends. Luca even learns a new hairstyle!

The boys wonder what it would be like to visit the human town of Portorosso. They imagine buying a real Vespa there and riding free.

Luca's parents find out he's been going above the surface and threaten to send him to live with his uncle in the deep sea. Luca runs away. He and Alberto swim to Portorosso!

The people of Portorosso do not like sea monsters. They even have a fountain showing a man slaying a creature from the ocean!

Ercole is the town bully. He only cares about his Vespa, his appearance, and hunting sea monsters. By accident, he almost reveals Luca's and Alberto's real identities!

A spunky girl named Giulia saves the boys from Ercole. She tells them all about the Portorosso Cup, an annual race that includes swimming, riding a bike, and eating pasta.

The three friends decide to team up for the race. Giulia won't have to do it alone, and the boys could use the prize money to buy a Vespa!

It's difficult for Luca and Alberto to keep their sea monster identities hidden in Portorosso. When they visit Giulia's home, they see equipment for hunting sea monsters on the wall.

Giulia's father, Massimo, looks tough, but the fisherman has a big heart. He loves his daughter and likes her new friends.

Giulia teaches Luca all about the stars and outer space.
Luca is amazed by everything she has learned at her human school.

Luca begins to see that there's more to life than living underwater or riding a Vespa. And for once, he's thinking about what *he* wants to do.

Chapter Twelve

"Hey, look who it is!" Ercole said, his voice full of mock camaraderie. "And with no Giulia to hide behind."

Luca watched as Ercole approached in the dark, Ciccio and Guido right behind him. He wanted to run, but Alberto had planted his feet. Luca knew there was no way his friend was going to leave.

"Something's fishy with you two," Ercole said. "I mean, besides the smell. You're hiding something."

"Is it that we're smarter than you?" Alberto said. "I mean, we're not *really* hiding that. It's just kinda obvious."

Ercole glared at Alberto. "You know, people think I'm a nice guy. Always joking around." He reached out and grabbed Alberto roughly, shoving him against a wall. "But really, I'm not."

"Stop!" Luca yelled.

Ercole nodded, and Ciccio and Guido took hold of

Alberto, keeping him against the wall. Then he shoved Luca to one side. "Wait your turn, Piccoletto."

Ercole turned his gaze to Alberto again. "I want to make myself very clear. This is my town, number one—" Then he punched Alberto. "And number two, I don't want you in it."

"I said *stop*!" Luca thundered, and to his disbelief, he found himself holding the harpoon that Ercole had thrown earlier. It was right up against Ercole's chest.

Ercole grinned and took a step closer to Luca. "Put that down, Piccoletto. You'll hurt yourself."

But Luca didn't put it down. "Let him go," he said, terrified.

With a nod from Ercole, Ciccio and Guido shoved Alberto at Luca.

"Go now," Ercole said. "Before I change my mind."

The two boys backed off, then ran. Luca tossed the harpoon to the side.

"Nobody wants you here, idioti!" Ercole shouted after them. "Keep running!"

"Why did you make him mad? We should have left!" Luca insisted.

Somehow, they had run all the way back to Giulia's house without anyone following them. Luca was out of breath and angry.

"We're fine!" Alberto said, breathing hard, too. "I had it under control. All you gotta do is follow my lead, remember?"

Before Luca could say anything, Alberto stormed into the backyard.

The following morning, Luca was rudely awakened by Giulia doing her trumpet imitation, again.

"Rise and shine!" she shouted.

That day's training regimen consisted of Alberto sitting in the family kitchen, filled with bowls and bowls of all kinds of pasta. And *eating* bowls and bowls of all kinds of pasta. With a fork.

Alberto was frustrated, but determined to master the fork. He would eat all the pasta necessary to get that Vespa.

After the pasta session, it was outside and on the streets for Luca to get in some bicycle practice. He was on the fish-cart bicycle, of course, struggling to stay ahead of some kids walking along, eating watermelon.

The boys were ridiculously tired from their day of training and, after dinner, promptly fell asleep.

They were awakened the following morning not by the sound of Giulia's mock trumpet, but by Massimo. "Buongiorno!" he hollered from the backyard. "Andiamo, dai!"

When the boys scrambled down the tree, they saw

the fish-cart bicycle waiting for Luca. And for Alberto? Massimo held up a butter knife. His own knife!

On the fishing boat, Alberto watched in amazement as Massimo pulled up the heavy fish net with one arm. He wanted to do it just like Giulia's father, so Alberto tried to pull a net from the water with one arm.

It was a *lot* harder than it looked.

As he pulled on the net, Alberto saw a shadow in the water. He recognized it instantly. It was a sea monster!

Before Alberto could do anything, Massimo was already in motion. For he, too, had seen the shadow, and reached for his harpoon. Alberto gasped as the fisherman hurled it into the water.

"Sea monster!" Massimo shouted.

A moment later, Massimo retrieved the harpoon, only to discover what he had captured was a large clump of seaweed. He sighed heavily—and so did Alberto.

Alberto was about to get back to pulling up the fishing net when he got a good, close look at one tattoo on Massimo's arm.

It was a sea monster, getting harpooned.

"Rise and shine! Only two days till the race!"

Luca could have sworn he heard Giulia calling to him

and Alberto from her window, but then again, he was so tired, it could just as easily have been some kind of waking dream. He resolved to get back to sleep even harder than before.

Unfortunately, Giulia, who *had* actually called them, wouldn't be so easily deterred. She marched right into the backyard and practically dragged both boys down from the hideout and into the house. Once inside, she handed the two zombie-like boys each a cup of hot, steaming something.

"Espresso," Giulia said.

Like robots, the boys took the cups. With one sip of the super-strong coffee, they perked right up. From that moment on, training intensified.

Luca was poring over the pages of a book called *Advanced Techniques in Cycling.* But he wasn't just reading it. He was cycling. At least, he was pedaling. Upside down. Lying on his back.

Nearby, Alberto was exercising his pasta-picking-up arm muscles, using Machiavelli as a reluctant weight.

As Giulia looked around, she began to think they really had a shot at winning this thing. And for once, she wouldn't be doing it alone.

Another day went by, and Luca was once again training on the bicycle. This time, he was out on the streets of

Portorosso. More confident than ever, Luca pedaled furiously, passing a group of kids eating gelato.

Someone else was watching Luca.

Ercole.

When the gelato kids called, "Go, Luca! You got it!" Ercole grimaced.

"Hey! Don't cheer for him!" Ercole screamed as the kids ran away in fear. "Argh! A casa!"

That night at dinner, Alberto was having a really rough time. He struggled to get pasta on his fork. It kept slipping off! The plate of spaghetti might as well have been a mountain, and he cursed the horrid thing.

Massimo noticed, and he patiently showed Alberto the precise way to twirl the fork and wrap the pasta.

Alberto sighed, then imitated Massimo's motions with the fork perfectly. His eyes lit up when he saw that he now had a massive forkful of twirled spaghetti.

Victory!

He shoved the spaghetti into his mouth and looked at Luca to share his joy.

But Luca didn't notice. He was too busy reading a book with Giulia.

Narrowing his eyes, Alberto grunted and returned to eating.

The next day, Daniela and Lorenzo once again wandered through the piazza, searching in vain for their son. They sat down at the fountain, feeling completely hopeless.

"I don't know, Lorenzo," Daniela said. "Was I too hard on Luca?"

"No. You were just trying to keep him safe," he said. "It's my fault. I wasn't paying enough attention to him."

"But I was the one who tried to send him away," Daniela insisted. "I just never in a million years would have thought he'd do this. It's like I don't even know who he is. . . ."

As her voice trailed off, Daniela stared into the distance, her eyes growing ever wider. There was a boy, pedaling a bicycle, with another boy and a girl.

"Dai forza! You can do it, Luca!" said the girl on the bicycle. "Go! Go!"

The boy on the bicycle looked just like—

"Luca!" Daniela cried.

Daniela took off running after the bicycle. Lorenzo was right behind her. But as fast as she could run, Luca on the bicycle was faster. He went down a side street and was gone.

Chapter Thirteen

"Where are we going?" Giulia asked.

Luca had turned the bicycle onto a different street. He thought for a second and said, "Uh, a shortcut!"

Giulia looked at Luca, impressed. "Steeper, rough terrain. I like it!"

Alberto rolled his eyes.

"Why aren't you training?" Giulia asked Alberto.

In response, Alberto pulled a big clump of pasta from his pocket and shoved it into his mouth. "I'm always training," he mumbled around the food.

As the bicycle reached the top of a hill, Luca looked thoroughly exhausted. He turned toward the bottom of the hill and saw no sign of them.

His parents.

He had seen them, back near the piazza, and in that moment, he'd panicked. That was why he had ridden so hard, so fast, and taken the "shortcut."

"Bravo, Luca," Giulia said. "That was your bestest yet!"

Then she pointed down the hill at a train that was leaving the Portorosso station and heading up the coast.

"Oh! Guys, look! That's the train to Genova!" she said.

"That goes to your school?" Luca asked.

Giulia nodded as Luca looked at the train longingly.

Alberto rolled his eyes again. *"Pffft,"* he said.

"I was wondering, actually," Luca said slowly. "Is your school open to . . . everyone?"

"Well, it costs a little money, but . . . I guess!" Giulia replied.

"Great," Alberto said. "Thank you, Giulia, for showing us the boring thing that takes us to the terrible place. Now can we focus on what matters? If we lose this race, we're not going anywhere."

Luca grasped the handlebars of the bicycle a little tighter, and looked down the hill.

"Santa Mozzarella, the downhill," he said softly.

"I know it looks scary. But here's what you need to know," Giulia advised.

"Would you stop bossing him around?" Alberto said, interrupting her.

"What is your problem?" Giulia demanded.

"I'm his friend! I know what he needs!" Alberto insisted.

"Oh, yeah? Well, then what does he need?"

Alberto moved in front of Luca on the bicycle and said,

"Me. We'll just ride it like we did on the island! Together! Andiamo!"

Alberto pushed off, taking everyone by surprise. The bicycle started down the hill, wobbling, weaving left and right, as Giulia and Luca shouted "No!" and "Alberto, stop!" The bicycle was totally out of control, going way too fast.

But whenever Luca protested, Alberto just said, "That's Bruno talking!"

"No, I'm pretty sure that's just me!" Luca replied.

But Alberto wouldn't brake for anything. And when Luca tried to take control of the bicycle, they ran into someone playing chess.

The boys continued to fight over control of the bicycle, and this time, they smashed into a guy carrying a crate full of lemons. Both Luca and Alberto ended up with a lemon in their mouth.

Just as they spit out the lemons, the bike came to a cliff.

And then it went over the cliff . . .

. . . where it hit the sea with a resounding *SPLASH.*

"Porca paletta. What was that?" Ercole wondered aloud. He had just heard the splash. Ciccio ran over to the water to scout things out.

Ciccio shrugged, then offered Ercole a bite of sandwich. Ercole knocked the thing out of his hands and barked,

"Not now, Ciccio!" He rose from his seat, harpoon in hand. "Eyes on the water! Move, move!"

Giulia had already reached a railing above, but Luca and Alberto were still underwater. Luca could see that Giulia was looking around in a panic, trying to find them.

But he also knew that he couldn't let her see them like this. Like sea monsters.

Reluctantly, he swam off, down the coast, away from Giulia. Alberto followed.

A little while later, Luca surfaced, and then Alberto's head bobbed up.

"Look," Alberto said, trying to explain his behavior. "I was just trying to show you how to do it right."

"You don't know how to do it right!" Luca shot back. They walked out of the water and onto shore. As they dried off, they transformed into their land monster selves.

"I got us down the hill, didn't I?"

"You crashed! Into the sea!"

"It's fine!" Alberto insisted.

"Nothing's fine! My parents just saw me!"

"Luca, your parents aren't here."

"You don't know what you're talking about!"

Alberto shook his head. "Look, this town is making you crazy. We just need to win that Vespa, and we get outta here."

Then he put his arm around Luca, attempting to make peace. But Luca wasn't having any part of it, and threw his arm off.

"It's not gonna be any different! I don't want to . . . ," Luca said. Then, summoning his strength, "I want to go to school."

"That again? We can't go to school!"

"You're just afraid you can't do it!"

"I'm not afraid," Alberto said. "You're the one who gets afraid." He shoved Luca.

Luca shoved back. "Shut up!" he said.

Then the fighting started.

"What happens when she sees you?" Alberto gasped as he got Luca in a hold. "When anyone sees you?"

Luca shoved Alberto off, but before the fight could resume, Giulia came running over.

"You're alive!" she shouted, and hugged them both. "Hey, you're never allowed on my bike again. Stick to food, big guy."

Giulia was just glad to see the boys, and was trying to make light of what had happened before. But she immediately sensed that something was wrong between them.

"Uh, what's going on?" she asked.

"Nothing," Alberto said. "Let's just get back to training."

"Actually, we have something to ask you," Luca said. "We were wondering . . . if we could come with you to your school?"

Giulia couldn't believe it. "Santo Pecorino! That's the best idea ever! Yes! Of course!"

Alberto was fuming. That was it. "Uh, Giulia, your school . . . does it take all kinds of people? I mean, what if some of them were . . . not human?"

"Alberto?" Luca said, utterly afraid that his friend was going to say something rash.

"What if some were, oh, I don't know, sea monsters?"

"Sea monsters?" Giulia repeated, not getting it.

"I doubt your school would even accept sea monsters, right?"

"Oh!" Luca said, erupting in a fake laugh. "Ha, ha! That's a weird joke, Alberto."

"Yeah, I know, it's kinda hard to imagine," Alberto said. "So let me just show you."

And Alberto fell into the water.

Luca screamed, "No!" but it was already too late.

Giulia was annoyed. "Ugh, come on—we don't have time to goof around."

But Luca told her to wait. A moment later, Alberto came out of the water.

As a sea monster.

Instantly, Giulia was afraid. "Don't hurt us!" she shouted.

"See?" Alberto said, happy to be right. "I knew this would hap—"

"Sea monster!" Luca screamed, pointing at Alberto.

"Luca?" Alberto asked, confused.

There were tears in Luca's eyes as he shook his head.

Giulia positioned herself between Luca and Alberto, and said, "Stay back."

Whatever it was that Luca was trying to do, he picked a really bad time to do it. Because at that moment, Ercole and his friends heard the shouts of "sea monster" and ran to see what was going on.

As they emerged over some rocks, harpoons in hand, Ercole shouted, "Sea monster! There it is!"

Ercole charged toward Alberto, screaming, "Ragazzi, now!"

Alberto shot Luca a look of utter disappointment and misery, then dove into the water. Ercole aimed his harpoon, throwing it into the sea.

"No!" Luca yelled.

But the harpoon missed, and Luca could do nothing but watch as Alberto swam away.

"Gah," Ercole said, then turned to face Luca and Giulia. "Idioti! You let it get away!" Then, looking at Ciccio and Guido, he said, "To the boat! We're gonna kill a sea monster!"

Giulia and Luca stood on the shore, watching as Ercole and his friends ran off.

Chapter Fourteen

"Ah, there you are! I made your favorite," Massimo said, holding a large pot full of pasta. "Trenette al pesto—"

Giulia and Luca entered the dining room, their faces looking anything but happy.

"Where's Alberto?" Massimo asked.

"Ah, he uh, he left, Signore Marcovaldo," Luca said.

Massimo set the pot down and walked over to grab his coat. "Do you know where he went?"

"No," Luca replied nervously. "But I don't think he wants anyone looking for him."

"Maybe not," Massimo said. "But just in case."

Massimo left the house, leaving Giulia and Luca to sit there in stunned silence.

"Okay. Well. The two of us can still do the race," Luca babbled, trying to fill the awkward silence.

"Luca, I—" Giulia began.

"You'll swim, you'll eat—you've done both before—and I'll do the ride."

"Luca—"

"I mean, that's allowed, right? It should be fine, we're still okay—"

"Luca!"

But Luca kept babbling. Finally, Giulia grabbed a glass from the table and splashed some water onto Luca's hands.

They transformed.

"'Sleeping under the fish,'" Giulia said, gritting her teeth. "Now I get it."

"I—I can explain," Luca said.

"Of all the places for sea monsters to visit—Portorosso? Have you seen this town?" Giulia pointed at the harpoons on the walls. "My father *hunts sea monsters*! Ugh, what were you guys thinking? Luca, you have to get out of here!"

Giulia pushed Luca toward the door.

"But I thought we were underdogs," he said.

"Do you think I *want* you to leave?" Giulia replied, anguish in her voice. "This is the happiest I've . . . look, it's just not worth it!"

"You don't understand—"

"No, I don't," Giulia said. "Risking your life? For a Vespa?"

"My parents were gonna send me away!" Luca said, near tears. "I was never gonna see him again! That's why we . . . did all of this."

Suddenly, Luca realized what he had done.

"But it's over now."

He went to the door. "Goodbye, Giulia. I'm sorry."

Then he was gone.

As Luca walked along the shore, he knew there was at least one thing he could do right. He could try to talk to Alberto.

He swam back to Alberto's hideout and climbed up. But as he called out Alberto's name, Luca was shocked to find the place had been completely trashed. The cool human stuff that Alberto had spent all that time collecting had been ripped from the shelves and strewn around the floor, broken.

"What are you doing here?" Alberto said coldly, looking down at Luca from the top of the stairs.

"I'm—I'm sorry," Luca said. "I never should have done that. I wish I could take it back."

"Yeah, whatever," Alberto said, not buying it. "You're sorry. Now *go away*."

Alberto turned, and Luca sighed. He stared at the wall where the Vespa poster had been, only to see that it had been torn away. And behind it, there were little tally marks on the wall that Luca hadn't seen before.

"What are those marks on the wall?" Luca asked quietly.

When he wouldn't answer, Luca became more insistent. "Alberto, tell me what they mean."

"I started when my dad left," Alberto replied.

Luca couldn't believe it.

"You were living here alone for that many days?"

"I just stopped counting after a while. He said I was old enough to be on my own," Alberto said quietly. "I just thought maybe he'd change his mind. Honestly, though, I get it. He's better off without me. You are, too."

"That's not true," Luca said.

"Yes, it is. You're not like me. You're the good kid. And I'm just the kid that ruins everything."

"Silenzio, Bruno!" Luca shouted. "That's just a dumb voice in your head. You taught me that."

"Well, I was wrong," Alberto said.

"And getting a Vespa—seeing the world . . ."

Alberto exploded. "Just let it go! Okay? Look, you and I should never have been friends in the first place."

"Don't say that. Alberto. . . ."

"Get outta here!" Alberto screamed. "I'm not gonna tell you again!"

Luca began to cry, but he refused to give up. "Okay, I'll go. I'll go win the race."

"What?"

"Yeah . . . yeah! And then the Vespa will be ours and we'll ride away, together!" Luca continued.

"Luca, that's crazy," Alberto said.

"Well, maybe *I'm* crazy!"

Then Luca ran right off the roof, shouting, "Take me, gravity!" He landed in a heap on the ground. He looked up and saw Alberto staring back at him.

"What are you doing?" Alberto asked.

"I'm okay! I'll be back tomorrow! I'm gonna fix this!" Luca said, running off.

Chapter Fifteen

The day of the race arrived.

And Luca had a plan.

"You want to split up your team?" Signora Marsigliese asked, incredulous.

Luca stood at the registration table, holding a rusty bicycle encrusted with barnacles. "Yes, if it's allowed," he said hopefully.

"Luca!"

He turned to see Giulia, who was on her way to the starting line. She ran over to him. "What are you doing here?"

"Don't worry," Luca said. "We'll race separately. You won't get in any trouble."

"You can if you want," Signora Marsigliese said with a shrug. "But I don't recommend it."

Before Giulia could stop him, Luca ran off. "Thank you!" he called out.

"But how are you gonna—I mean, what happens when— *You can't swim!*" Giulia shouted at Luca.

Giulia looked back at Signora Marsigliese, who gazed at her sympathetically. "Alone again?" she said.

Giulia scowled.

Daniela and Lorenzo were still wandering the streets of Portorosso, looking for their son. They had spotted Luca a couple of times, but hadn't come close to actually talking to him.

Suddenly, the priest grabbed them and pinned ribbons on their chests. Then he shoved them down behind a table. "Volunteers!" the man said. "You're late!"

Then Daniela looked at the table and saw rows of water cups. Apparently, this was all set up for the big race they had been hearing about, the one that was happening today. The priest must want them to be judges of some kind. This was perfect!

"One cup for each kid," the priest said.

"Yeah, yeah, yeah. One cup per kid. Got it," Daniela replied.

Lorenzo wasn't sure of what was happening, but he knew enough to trust Daniela, so he followed her lead.

"Ohhh . . . yes!" Lorenzo said.

Then the priest handed them a bucket with a scrub brush. "For when Giulia . . . you know."

They did not know. And something told Daniela they did not want to know.

Giulia waited at the starting line, unsure of how this was all going to work out. She looked around but saw no sign of Luca. Her eyes drifted to the crowd of people that had assembled, and she smiled when she saw her father with Machiavelli.

"Forza, Giulietta!" her father hollered.

Then Ciccio and Ercole walked right up next to her. Ercole took out a container and poured something all over Ciccio.

"Ciccio, hold still," Ercole said, annoyed. Then he turned to look at Giulia. "Olio d'olivia." Olive oil. "He will cut through the water like a knife. An oily knife."

At that moment, both Giulia and Ercole spotted Luca. He stomped over to the starting line, wearing a full-body diving suit that he had taken from Alberto.

"Oh, this makes me laugh," Ercole said. "HA, HA, HA. I guess even your terrible friends don't want to be friends."

Luca looked at everyone assembled at the starting line, but mostly Giulia and Ercole.

"Luca! This is a very bad idea!" Giulia yelled.

"Hey! Vagrant! Can't afford a proper swimsuit?" Ercole jabbed.

"Signore e Signori!" Signora Marsigliese called out. "The

Portorosso Cup is about to begin! We know there've been a few sightings lately, but fear not! If any sea monsters show up today—we're ready for them!"

She turned and pointed to the harbor, at the fishermen in the boats, with their nets and their harpoons.

Luca gasped. He looked over at Giulia, and she made a motion that said *"Get out of here now!"*

But he didn't.

"Swimmers, take your mark!" Signora Marsigliese said.

Taking a deep breath, Luca attached the helmet to his suit.

Then the sound of the starting pistol echoed in his helmet, and all the contestants dove into the water!

All of them, that is, except Luca.

He just stood there, frozen, his pulse quickening, head shaking. Could he do this? He couldn't do this. There was no way.

No, wait. That was Bruno talking. *"Silenzio, Bruno."*

Then Luca dove into the water.

Giulia was determined to win the race, and was swimming with all the heart she had to give. But Ciccio was ahead of her, and the other competitors, too. She wondered if maybe that olive oil really did give him an advantage.

But then she noticed that fish started to swarm around Ciccio. And they weren't leaving him alone.

Aha! Giulia thought. The olive oil must have been attracting the fish. Maybe they were hungry. Maybe they would . . . eat Ciccio? There was no way they could be so lucky.

Behind her, and behind everyone else, was Luca. He was also underneath them. The heavy diving suit he wore was meant not for swimming, but for walking on the ocean floor! So there he was, trudging along. No matter how much effort he put in, no matter how hard he tried to move forward, he just couldn't keep up with the group.

Even worse, Luca noticed that the suit had developed a leak. He picked up the pace, exerting even more effort.

Above, Giulia had rounded the buoy and was already swimming back to shore. She passed Ciccio, who was having great difficulty in the water now, as fish were nipping at his skin. The fish actually *were* trying to eat Ciccio!

Ciccio freaked out. The fish were really only nipping at him a little, in a way that couldn't possibly do him any harm, but Ciccio didn't seem to realize this.

Giulia was the first one out of the water, and she ran right past Ercole. He looked back at the water and screamed, "Swim, Ciccio! C'mon! Swim!"

Running right to the pasta stage, Giulia sat herself down, ready to go. The surprise pasta was unveiled, a narrow flat noodle, and she exclaimed, "Ha, ha! Trenette!"

Meanwhile, beneath the surface, Luca's suit was filling

with water as he continued to move forward, one soggy step at a time.

Back on the shore, the judges were getting nervous. They knew that Luca was still in the water, and they weren't sure what to do. Maybe it was time to go in after him?

They were just about to send people in to fetch him when he finally emerged from the water! He slogged his way past Ercole, who, of course, being a complete jerk, tripped him.

Luca fell, and ducked under a table. He wiggled his way out of the heavy diving suit and used the tablecloth to dry himself off. A moment later, he transformed into his land monster form and took a seat at the table.

He was sitting next to Giulia! She rolled her eyes at him like she couldn't believe what he was doing and how dangerous it was.

Luca stared at the plate in front of him, piled with pasta that looked like wide ribbons. He tried to get some on his fork, but it just wasn't working.

"Come on, come on . . . ," he said.

Giulia was eating as fast as she could, her mouth crammed full of pasta. She watched him fumble with the fork. She couldn't take it anymore, and in a very exaggerated way, showed him how to twirl the pasta around the fork to eat it.

"Thank you!" Luca said.

"Don't thank me!" Giulia said, her mouth still full.

And just then, Ciccio emerged from the water, screaming because little fish were still hanging on to his oil-soaked skin, still nibbling.

"Stop crying! Tag Guido!" Ercole yelled, as Ciccio screamed. "Imbecile!"

Ciccio managed to do that as Ercole pushed Guido over to the pasta competition. "Andiamo! Run! Run!"

Guido sat down and started to eat like a maniac.

But Giulia had already finished. She slammed her fork onto the table, and the crowd went wild!

Alberto sat there in his hideout, looking out the window. In the distance, he could see Portorosso. He knew the race was happening right now. The race that he was supposed to be taking part in, along with Luca and Giulia.

Yet, here he was. Sitting in his hideout.

Alone.

His eyes drifted to the sky above, and he noticed the dark clouds rolling in. A storm. With a storm came rain.

Alberto groaned.

"Finito!" Giulia cried as she stood up from the pasta table. Immediately, she grabbed her stomach. She hobbled over to the bicycles, groaning with each step. Ercole glared at her angrily as she got on and rode off.

"Per mille cavoli!" Ercole screamed. "Guido! *Faster!*"

And faster was exactly what Luca was trying to be. He was stabbing and twirling pasta as quickly as he could and eating it as he watched the other kids finish their dishes, stand up, and tag their partners for the bicycle portion of the race.

Luca was way behind. But if there was any saving grace to this situation, so was Ercole! There he stood, forcefully shoving pasta into Guido's mouth.

"Eat, idiota! Più veloce!"

Guido groaned in response.

Another kid who had just finished eating, face covered in pasta sauce, was slumped against a wall. He pointed at Ercole and Guido. "Hey! That's not allowed!"

"He's done!" Ercole announced, ignoring the kid as he slammed the fork onto the table, picked up Guido's hand, and used it to slap his own hand, tagging Ercole into the race. Ercole sprinted to his bicycle and got on.

And, in last place, Luca managed to slurp up the final piece of pasta on his plate. He high-fived himself, dropped the fork, and ran to his bicycle.

Then he let out a loud burp and rode away.

Chapter Sixteen

Kids whizzed by on their bicycles as Daniela and Lorenzo attempted to hand out the cups of water. It wasn't easy, because they were moving so fast! And, frankly, they were still getting used to the sensation of moving around in air instead of water.

"He's gotta be here somewhere," Daniela said, scanning the competitors.

"Thirsty? Water, anyone?" Lorenzo said, trying to do his job.

But the kids recognized Daniela and Lorenzo as the adults who had been ambushing and splashing them for days. They dodged the water cups, shouting and yelling.

"Not again!"

"Please don't!"

"Nooooo!"

At last, Daniela spotted a kid at the end of the racers. "That's him!" she said, her voice rising. "Luca! Stop!"

The couple lunged for him, but Luca screamed and swerved away from his parents. "Sorry, Mom! Sorry, Dad!" he called out as he pedaled on. "I have to do this!"

They ran after him, but Luca was much too fast.

"Get back here right now!" Lorenzo yelled.

Daniela was too impressed by her son's amazing bicycling abilities to yell. "Wow, he's fast!" was all she could think to say.

Luca was tearing up the streets, making up the ground he had lost from the swimming and eating portions of the competition. He passed one racer, and then another, and another!

There came a rumbling sound in the distance, and Luca allowed his eyes to drift upward for just a second—dark clouds were rolling in. He hoped the race would end before anything happened. Then he trained his eyes forward, where he saw Giulia, riding up in front of the pack. He could have sworn that he saw her cover her mouth, like she was trying to prevent herself from getting sick.

That was when Ercole passed her. Adding insult to injury, he slapped the top of her helmet.

"Oops!" he said in a mocking tone. "Scusa!"

Giulia growled. "I'll catch you on the downhill!"

"Spewlia, you never even made it to the downhill," Ercole laughed.

Pleased with his performance and sure of his victory, Ercole slowed down for a moment. He even primped his hair in preparation for the cameras when he crossed the finish line first.

So it came as an utter, horrible shock when he saw *Luca* pass him!

"What!" Ercole screamed. "Impossible! He's cheating! Arbitro! Arbitro!"

Luca said nothing. He just kept right on pedaling, heading up the hill, pumping his legs as hard as he could.

For the first time in the entire race, Luca thought that maybe, just maybe, he might be able to win!

And then a drop of rain fell on his hand.

"No, no, no, no, no!" Luca said as he looked down and saw the scales appear.

The rain began to fall in the piazza, and the onlookers took out their umbrellas and opened them. Massimo was there, watching curiously as someone grabbed one of the larger café umbrellas. That was certainly unusual.

Even more unusual, whoever had taken the café umbrella was now headed down the street with it.

He wondered what was going on.

Even with the rain, Luca refused to give up. He kept pedaling, even harder than he had before, as if he were in a race against the rain itself. With surprising speed, he made it to the top of the hill.

But now the rain turned into a downpour. Luca had no choice but to pull his bicycle over to the side of the road and duck under an awning—right before the downhill portion of the race.

"Oh, not now," Luca moaned. "Come on, come on, come on! I'm so close! Please stop!"

Luca pleaded with the rain, but it was no use. He might as well have been talking to a sky full of fish.

Then something made him look up.

He saw Alberto running toward him, carrying a huge umbrella like one they had seen at the cafés down at the piazza!

"Luca!" he called. "Just stay right there!"

"Alberto," Luca said, stunned.

"I'm coming for you!"

At that moment, Ercole came over the hill on his bicycle. He slowed down when he saw Luca under the awning.

"What's wrong, Piccoletto? Afraid of a little rain?" But Ercole wasn't done yet. "And there's the other one. For the last time, you two don't belong here. Get out of my town."

Ercole rode by and kicked Alberto, knocking him over. The umbrella went flying as Alberto rolled toward Luca. He got up right away, but it was too late—he had already gotten wet, and was now revealed to be a sea monster!

Ercole suddenly stopped. "Ahhhhh!" he screamed. "Sea monster! Right there!"

The crowd gasped at the sight of the sea monster in their midst, and so did the other racers.

Ercole yelled down the hill, "Ciccio! My harpoon! Veloce!"

Luca looked at Alberto. He was still under the awning, dry, looking at Alberto in his sea monster form, standing in the rain.

Giulia had now joined them on the hill and saw what was happening. She hit her brakes.

Luca looked at Alberto and took a step toward him.

"No, stop!" Alberto said, and backed away. "Just stay there! You're still okay." Then he looked at the crowd and ran at them, shouting, *"Andiamooooo!"*

"Alberto, wait!" Luca yelled, but there was nothing he could do to stop his friend now.

Cries of "Sea monster!" and "Stop that thing!" erupted from the mass of people. Several people in the crowd threw a net, capturing Alberto, who fell to the ground, helpless.

"Don't let it get away!" someone yelled.

"No!" Luca said, and with great determination, he pedaled his bike out into the rain. Immediately, he transformed into his sea monster self.

It was the first time that Giulia had seen Luca as a sea monster. "Santa Ricotta!" she said.

Luca rode right through the crowd that had gathered

around the trapped Alberto. Then he held out his hand and pulled Alberto onto the bicycle.

"What?" Ercole shouted, unable to process what was happening.

Luca pedaled down the hill as Alberto tossed the net aside.

"Whoa! You really are crazy!" Alberto said.

"Yeah, and I learned it from you!" Luca replied.

Alberto hugged Luca.

"Let's get to the water," Luca said as they rode past Ercole. A second later, Ciccio handed a harpoon to Ercole.

"No, Ciccio!" Ercole yelled, angry at his friend's lack of timing. He raced down the hill after Luca and Alberto, harpoon in hand.

Giulia was right behind them.

Chapter Seventeen

"Out of the way!" Ercole shouted, hot on the heels of Luca and Alberto. One way or another, he was going to get those sea monsters!

He hoisted his harpoon, ready to throw. This was the moment Ercole had been waiting for!

Alberto glanced over his shoulder and saw what was coming. "Luca!" he said, and forced his friend to swerve, suddenly going off course. The bicycle veered right into an apartment, over a balcony, and down a flight of stairs.

There was a lot of screaming as they went from the stairs and onto the roof of an apartment building. They jumped off the roof, and somehow, miraculously, ended up back on the racecourse, right behind Ercole and Giulia!

"Son!"

Luca turned his head briefly as he saw his father and mother standing by the side of the road under a tarp.

"You shoulda left when I told you," Ercole said, readying his harpoon. "Now I gotta kill some sea monsters!"

Luca leaned to one side, transferring his weight as he tried to evade Ercole.

But Ercole was closing in fast.

Ercole and that horrible harpoon.

Then Giulia caught up with Ercole.

"So long, evil empire of injustice," she muttered.

The next thing Ercole knew, Giulia collided with him, and their bicycles went flying! Ercole let go of the harpoon as they crashed and hit the ground.

Giulia sat up, woozy, and gave Luca and Alberto a thumbs-up. Then she grabbed her arm and held it close to her body. She was hurt!

Luca knew what he had to do. He hit the brakes and the bicycle came to a halt.

Massimo stood in the crowd in the piazza, staring at the sea monster boys in astonishment.

"Mostri marini . . . Give me that!" he shouted, grabbing a harpoon.

Meanwhile, both Luca and Alberto hopped off the bicycle and ran back to help Giulia off the ground. "Giulia!" Alberto said, his voice full of concern.

"Are you all right?" Luca asked.

"Guys . . . I'm okay," she said, a little dazed by seeing her two friends in sea monster form. The boys lifted Giulia, carrying her all the way into the piazza. But when they entered, they were met by Massimo and a wall of fishermen wielding nets and harpoons. The mob surrounded the children.

"Sea monster!" Massimo shouted. "Giulietta?"

"Papá . . . I—"

Alberto looked up at Massimo hopefully, but Massimo was frozen. Alberto's smile faded as the rest of the fishermen closed in around them.

One of the fishermen laughed. "You're not going anywhere."

Ercole stormed through the crowd, armed with his harpoon.

"I saw them first! The reward is mine!" he shouted, stepping into the circle of fishermen.

This time, Luca stood up to him.

"We're not afraid of you!" Luca said.

"No. But we're afraid of *you*." Ercole said. "Everyone is horrified and disgusted by you. Because *you* are monsters."

"There he is! Luca!" Daniella shouted as she and Lorenzo entered the piazza.

"Let us through!" Lorenzo said. The mob was closing in tighter and tighter.

"Stop! They're not monsters!" Giulia shouted.

"Yeah? Who are they, then?" Ercole snarled.

"I know who they are," Massimo spoke, silencing the crowd.

The fishermen parted, allowing Massimo to step closer. Gently, he took Alberto's hand and said, "They are Luca and Alberto. And they are . . . the winners!" He raised Alberto's hand in the air.

A ripple of confusion ran through the piazza.

"What?" Luca asked.

Alberto couldn't believe what he was hearing. "Really?"

"They can't be the winners. They are not even . . . people!" Ercole said.

Massimo ignored him.

"Signora?" he continued, nodding at Luca and Alberto's bicycle, which was lying across the finish line. Signora Marsigliese studied it closely, deliberated for a moment, and then shrugged.

"Technically . . . legally . . . yes," Signora Marsigliese said.

Luca gazed around at the crowd, which was murmuring in confusion. Massimo looked sternly at the fishermen until they lowered their harpoons. Some shook their heads in disgust, and some began to leave, but Ercole wasn't finished.

"Who cares if they won? They're sea monsters!"

While Ercole was preoccupied, Giulia snatched his harpoon and handed it to Alberto and Luca. Together, they snapped it in half.

"Ciccio! Guido! Another harpoon! Velocemente!" Ercole demanded. When they didn't obey right away, he was infuriated. "Argh, idioti! Be useful for once in your pathetic lives!"

"Guido," Ciccio said.

"Ciccio," Guido replied, as if each understood exactly, precisely, what the other was thinking.

And so they walked right over to Ercole, picked him up, and tossed him directly into the fountain.

"Gahhh!" Ercole said in a panic. "I can't swim!"

He thrashed in the shallow water, in danger of damaging absolutely nothing other than his pride.

But Ciccio wasn't done. He pulled out Ercole's wool sweater and threw it in after him.

"Oops," Ciccio said.

Guido looked at Ercole, stuck out his tongue, and blew perhaps the most elegant raspberry in the history of raspberries: *"Thhhhppppbbbbbttt."*

"It's over," Giulia said, watching from afar. "The reign of terror . . . it's finally over!"

"Luca!"

Turning his head at the sound of his name, Luca smiled as his mother and father broke through the crowd and wrapped him in the tightest of hugs.

Of course, as it was raining, Daniela and Lorenzo were now fully revealed as sea monsters, too.

"Luca, you had us worried half to death," Daniela started, "and you must never do that again. And you raced your little tail off, and kicked so much human butt, and I'm so proud of you, and I'm so mad at you!"

"I'm sorry!" Luca said.

Daniela hugged him even closer. Lorenzo joined in. The crowd watched in astonishment as the sea monsters hugged their sea monster kid. Some of them softened at the sight. One human parent, watching them, hugged their own child close.

"Signore e Signori, the winners of this year's Portorosso Cup . . . the Underdogs!" Signora Marsigliese announced, walking up to the kids with a trophy. "Bravissimi!"

The kids cheered, finally realizing it was real. They were the winners of the Portorosso Cup!

The kids of Portorosso started celebrating, too.

"Go, Underdogs!"

"Ercole lost!"

"I know sea monsters!"

The two older women the boys had encountered when they'd first come to town—the ones Luca had accidentally called stupido—tossed their umbrellas aside. The rain hit their skin, revealing that they were sea monsters, too! It looked like Luca and Alberto hadn't been the only sea monsters hiding in plain sight!

Chapter Eighteen

Luca and Alberto had their Vespa at last. The rickety wheels rolled along the cobblestones as kids from town ran behind them.

"Whoa! They got a Vespa?"

"No way!"

"Ha, ha, ha! Feast your eyes! On the greatest Vespa the world has ever seen!" Alberto shouted.

Giulia and Luca cheered.

Alberto zoomed into the garden when Massimo was serving dinner. The Vespa made a horrendous coughing sound as parts fell off it.

"Perfect," Alberto said proudly.

Massimo smiled and served pasta to his guests, Daniela and Lorenzo . . . and Luca's grandma, who was also there, incredibly.

"Prego. Mangiate, mangiate!" Massimo said. Then, when he saw Grandma, he added, "Signora."

"Grazie," Grandma said, taking the pasta.

"Mom? What are you doing here?" Daniela asked.

"I come to town most weekends," Grandma replied.

Daniela laughed and watched her son as he talked to Giulia and Alberto. He seemed so happy, so carefree.

"What he did today was amazing," Daniela said. "But we can't let him stay in this world. Can we?"

"Some people, they'll never accept him," Grandma said, eating her pasta. "But some will. And he seems to know how to find the good ones."

"So where will you go first?" Giulia asked.

"We're gonna stick around here for a bit," Alberto said. "We gotta fix this thing up before we take it across the entire Earth."

"Okay. Just don't forget to . . . pack. Santa Gorgonzola!" Giulia said, suddenly realizing something very important. "I need to pack! For school!"

"Oh, yeah!" Luca said wistfully. "For school. You're gonna learn so much."

"I can leave you some books. . . ."

"You can?" Luca cried. "Come on, Alberto!"

Luca followed Giulia, and Alberto watched him go inside. He smiled, happy for his friend. Then his eyes went to the Vespa, and a thought came over him.

It was early in the morning, and the Portorosso train station was anything but crowded. Massimo had gotten Giulia to the station early, not wanting to risk her being late and missing her ride.

"And you have your lunch for the train?" Massimo said, looking at his daughter and her bags.

"Si," Giulia confirmed.

"Sweater if it gets cold?"

"For the millionth time, si," Giulia said. "I love you, too, Papá."

Then she gave her father a big hug and turned to see Alberto and Luca.

"Santa Mozzarella," Giulia said. "We did it!"

Alberto grinned as Giulia wrapped her arms around him and Luca, hugging them both.

"Ciao, Giulia," Luca said, and he watched as she boarded the train. Tears came to his eyes.

As Giulia disappeared inside, she called out, "Ciao, ragazzi! A presto."

Luca wiped his tears, then faced Alberto. "Well, let's go fix up our Vespa."

Alberto looked at his friend. He had a piece of paper in hand. "Yeah," he said. "About that. Uhh, crazy thing. I . . . might have sold it."

Alberto handed the paper to Luca.

It was a train ticket.

To Genova.

"What are you talking about?" Luca said. He looked at the ticket in his hand, not quite sure what was happening. And when he looked up, he saw that his parents and his grandma had arrived on the train platform! Carrying a bag, they walked over to Luca.

"Mom? Dad? Grandma?" Luca said. "What's going on?"

Daniela spoke first "*If.* You promise to write to us every single day, and be as safe as possible, and I mean safer than safe . . . you can go to school."

"I can?" Luca said, in shock.

"It's all arranged, actually," Lorenzo said. "You'd stay with Giulia and her mom."

"Your friend talked them into it. Wasn't easy," Grandma added.

Luca looked at Alberto, who shrugged. He couldn't believe Alberto had done that for him!

"Luca? Do you promise?" Daniela repeated.

"Yes! Yes, I promise!" Luca shouted.

He hugged everyone, and was so overcome, all he could manage to say was a heartfelt "Thank you."

"Just remember we are always here for you," Daniela said, reaching to fix Luca's hair, then catching herself. "Okay?"

"Hey. Look me in the eye," Luca said. "You know I love you. Right?"

"I know," Daniela said.

Then Luca kissed his mom and said, "Come on, Alberto! The train's gonna leave!"

"Oh, ah, hang on," Alberto replied.

Luca had already run down the platform and toward the train door when he noticed that Alberto had no bag with him. Nothing.

"Where's your stuff?" Luca asked.

"Yeah, well. You see . . . ," Alberto tried to explain.

"You *are* coming, right?"

"I would," Alberto said. "But Massimo asked if I wanted to stick around, move in, maybe . . . and I just thought, ah . . . I think he needs me. You know?"

Luca stood next to the train door, not sure what he should do next. "I can't do it without you" was all he could say.

Then Alberto handed Luca another piece of paper. Something that had been taped back together. It was a drawing he had made of the two of them.

"But you're never without me," Alberto said. "The next time you jump off a cliff, or tell Bruno to quit bothering you, that's me."

"How am I gonna know you're okay?"

Alberto wrapped Luca in his arms. "You got me off the island, Luca," Alberto said. "I'm okay."

The train was about to leave, so Luca slowly climbed the

steps of the train just as rain began to fall on the covered platform.

The two boys shook hands. The train pulled away from the station, with Alberto running alongside. When he reached the edge of the platform, Alberto jumped off into the rain, transforming into his sea monster self.

"Wooooo! Go, Luca, go!" Alberto shouted as Luca watched his friend grow smaller and smaller.

Luca kept looking until he couldn't see Alberto anymore. The train entered a dark tunnel, and for just a few minutes, Luca sat there, alone with his thoughts.

When the train emerged from the tunnel, Luca saw the hills that overlooked the sea. He leaned out into the rain and transformed into his sea monster form.

Luca took one last look at Portorosso, then ducked inside, ready to catch up to Giulia and greet the bright future that was just a train ride away.